Leah shook her head adamantly. "I'm not jealous! Sometimes you can be so blind, Katrina! I suppose you didn't see the way Annie was batting her eyelashes at Michael on the walk back, when she invited him to go to that dance in Rose Park Friday night."

"Maybe I didn't see that," Katrina confessed. "But I did see the way Michael was looking at her, and she didn't have to do much to get his attention. She's incredibly pretty. Just because she was nice to him doesn't mean she was flirting with him. And even if she was, why do you care? Would you have been happier if she had ignored Michael and made him miserable?"

"Maybe," Leah told her as she pulled back her covers. Then she paused before getting into bed. "You know, it really hurts to have you side against me, Katrina. I thought we were friends."

"Of course we're friends! But I like Annie, too. Anyway, I'm not taking sides because I don't think there are any sides to take." Katrina walked over to her own bed and sat down. "Maybe you're the one who feels competitive with Annie, Leah. Maybe that's why a few little things she's said or done are suddenly bothering you so much. Have you stopped to consider that?"

SUMMER DANCE

Satin Slippers #12

Elizabeth Bernard

FAWCETT GIRLS ONLY • NEW YORK

RLI: $\dfrac{\text{VL 7 \& up}}{\text{IL 8 \& up}}$

A Fawcett Girls Only Book
Published by Ballantine Books
Copyright © 1989 by Cloverdale Press, Inc.

Library of Congress Catalog Card Number: 89-91226

ISBN 0-449-14548-4

Manufactured in the United States of America

First Edition: September 1989

*For Michelle Louise Kelly and that summer
so long ago, it seems like yesterday.*

"That's your flight, Kay," Leah Stephenson said. She nodded her head at the loudspeaker, where a smooth female voice had just finished announcing flight 72 for New York City. Leah gave Kay Larkin a quick hug.

Leah hated saying good-bye, and she felt she'd had to do it far too often during the past year. First it had been good-bye to her mother, then to her best friend, Chrissy Morely, and her longtime ballet teacher, Hannah Greene, when she'd left her hometown of San Lorenzo, California, to attend the San Francisco Ballet Academy.

Since then Leah had had to say a constant stream of good-byes: one to her dynamic partner, James Cummings; one to her dear friend and fellow student, Alexandra Sorokin; and even one to her first real boyfriend, Peter Forrest. But undoubtedly the most painful good-bye of all had been the one Leah had said to SFBA itself following the injury she'd sustained backstage while warming up for her part in Madame Preston's birthday gala. Luckily that good-bye had turned out to be only temporary. Leah had gone back to the Academy on her sixteenth birthday in May.

Now it was mid-July, and Leah was dancing more strongly than ever.

Kay turned to Katrina Gray and gave her an affectionate hug as well. After taking a step back and looking first at Leah and then at Katrina, as if she was trying to memorize their faces, Kay smiled weakly.

"I wish we were all going to the same place," she said. "I'll miss you both so much. Promise you'll write."

"I'll write," Leah swore, "but you have to write back!"

Leah hoped she sounded more cheerful than she felt. Ever since Alex left SFBA to go to college, Kay had been Leah's best friend there. And even though she was thrilled about going to Summer Dance in Greenfield, Vermont, with Madame Preston, the Academy's director, Katrina, Michael Litvak, and Kenny Rotolo, she was really going to miss Kay a lot.

"I will," Kay assured Leah, picking up her bright red dance bag.

"I'll write you, too, Kay," Katrina vowed, her soft brown eyes sparkling from beneath her bangs.

Kay hiked her dance bag higher on her slender shoulder. Then she made a quick little turn and hurried toward the line of boarding passengers.

"We better go back to the gate and find Madame Preston," Katrina suggested. "We wouldn't want to miss our own flight."

Minutes later Leah and Katrina spotted Michael and Kenny. The boys were leaning against a railing, looking out the tall airport windows at the planes. Seeing their familiar faces made Leah smile.

She felt so lucky to have so many good friends at SFBA.

"There you are," Kenny said once the girls had joined them. "Did Kay get on her flight to New York?"

Katrina nodded. "It was kind of sad to see her go, even though she'll be in a fantastic program and everything. I mean, what could be more perfect for Kay than two weeks with Dana Daniels's avant-garde dance troupe?"

"Nothing," Michael agreed. "But it's time to quit thinking about Kay and start thinking about *our* trip."

"Right on, Michael." Kenny patted the taller boy on the back.

"The Summer Dance festival is going to be great!" Leah exclaimed. "Not only are we going to *study* with some of the most famous classical ballet dancers, we're going to get to dance with them onstage!"

"Three performances a week is what Madame Preston told me when she asked me to go," Michael said enthusiastically. Then, reaching into the side pocket of his dance bag, he produced a brochure and waved it in front of Leah. "Look at this. I got it from that travel agency near the Academy. Dancing isn't the only thing going on in Greenfield. It's a regular resort town. We're going to have a blast!"

Stepping closer to Michael, Leah looked down at the brightly colored brochure. She saw photograph after photograph of beautiful tree-covered hills. There was a ski area that offered hiking during the summer, a quaint-looking park, and a fabulous estate named Ado that served as an artists' retreat.

"Oh, look!" Leah cried. She pointed at the brochure with her index finger. "There's a picture of the Greenfield Performing Arts Center, where we'll be performing!" Katrina and Kenny crowded in next to Leah to get a closer look.

"And when we aren't dancing, we can go hiking and swimming," Michael suggested. "There's a movie theater and a couple of different coffee houses, and look at this country inn."

"And shopping," Katrina added. "I've been to Greenfield before, you know—I don't live very far away from it."

"Whoa!" Leah cried. "Aren't you all forgetting the classes we'll be taking? We might be too busy for all these other plans you guys are making. After all, we'll only be in Vermont for two weeks."

"There will be time for everything," Michael predicted. "At least for everything important. Right, Ken?"

"Right," Kenny agreed. "I can't wait to see Katrina's farm. Madame finally gave her permission, didn't she?"

Katrina nodded. "She talked it over with my parents first. She had a few conditions, but she said it was okay. I can't wait to show everyone around, either. You guys are going to love Vermont. It's really different from California in a lot of ways."

Leah felt like pirouetting around the crowded waiting room just to burn off some of the growing excitement she felt. As much as she loved California, Leah was looking forward to seeing what the Northeast looked like.

"You'll have to be our guide, then, Katrina," Kenny said, tugging affectionately on one of Katrina's braids. Katrina blushed.

Suddenly Leah frowned. "Isn't our plane supposed to be boarding now?" She nodded at the large clock on the terminal wall. "Where's Madame Preston?"

"She told us she had to make a phone call," Kenny replied. "Something about checking on her accommodations in Greenfield, I think."

"She'll probably be back in a minute or two," Michael said. "Don't worry, Leah. We'll be getting on the plane any minute now."

"Maybe we should get in line," Leah suggested anxiously. "Don't the airlines sometimes overbook flights?"

Michael slipped a protective arm around Leah and gave her a reassuring squeeze. "Don't worry, little lady," he said, imitating a cowboy. "I'll get you on that plane."

Leah giggled as she shrugged out of Michael's embrace. "You're my dance partner, Michael Litvak, not my hero."

Michael ran his fingers through his thick brown hair. "I actually consider myself both," he told her, sounding a little hurt.

"I don't really need someone to protect me," Leah said. "I can take care of myself." She smiled at Michael. Leah was most often paired with Michael during pas de deux class at the Academy, and according to Madame Preston, she'd also be dancing with him in pas de deux workshop at Summer Dance. There was certainly a closeness that came from that. But sometimes Leah had the uncomfortable feeling that Michael wanted them to be even closer than they already were.

"You are my favorite partner, though," she assured him. They had been dancing especially well together since Leah's recovery. Leah suspected that that was why Madame Preston had chosen them to go to Summer Dance with her. Madame was already talking about the two of them learning the romantic ballet *Giselle* in her pas de deux class in the fall. Obviously Madame's plans for Michael and Leah were long-range, and Leah was pleased about that.

Michael brightened. "That's right. And you're mine."

"Hey, you two, break it up, will you?" Kenny teased. "You're getting a little too sappy for me. I'm going to hit the soda machine I saw around the corner over there. Anybody interested in going with me?"

"I am! You girls better stay here, in case Madame comes back looking for us. Can I bring you anything, Leah?" Michael offered. "My treat."

Leah shook her head. "No, thanks."

Once the boys walked away, Katrina poked Leah in the ribs with her elbow. "Michael just doesn't give up, does he?"

"What are you talking about?" Leah asked.

"That crush he's got on you. You'd think he'd give up. But he doesn't, even though I've never seen you give him the least bit of encouragement. I mean, you're nice to him and everything, but you don't even flirt back when he flirts with you."

Leah shook her head and sighed. "I do know what you mean, and it isn't that I don't like Michael. I'm just not interested in anyone that way right now. I'm too busy dancing for that."

"Then I suppose Michael's right not to give up on you," Katrina commented. "You might just change your mind someday."

Leah was about to protest, when the boys reappeared.

"Did they call our flight yet?" Kenny asked.

Leah nodded. "They just announced that it was ready for boarding."

"We better get in line, then," Michael said.

"There's Madame," Katrina pointed out as they joined the people waiting to get on the plane to Boston. The Academy director was up in front, along with first-class passengers. She caught Leah's eye and waved.

"I guess Madame's sitting in first class," Michael told the others. "Apparently the patrons think Madame deserves special treatment."

"I think we *all* deserve special treatment," Kay commented.

Katrina ruffled Kenny's short, spiky hair. "Someday, maybe. But not this trip. We're still first-year students. It's going to be a while before we're members of a company, never mind important enough members to get first-class tickets."

"One day, though, when we're principal dancers in major companies, we'll *all* be traveling first-class," Michael said enthusiastically.

Leah showed the stewardess her boarding pass and began making her way down the narrow aisle of the airplane. With each step Leah felt the same kind of mounting excitement she always felt before getting onstage to dance. Greenfield, here I come, she thought to herself.

Leah glanced down at her boarding pass. "Here are Katrina and my seats," she told the boys. Then, looking down at Michael's pass, she added, "I think you guys are farther back."

Leah settled into the window seat, stowing all her carry-on luggage under the seat in front of her. Since it was Leah's first time in the air, Katrina had graciously offered to take the aisle seat so that Leah would have the view.

"It's just too bad," Katrina said as she sat down and buckled her seat belt.

"What's too bad?" Leah asked.

"The fact that you don't like Michael. I think you'd make as great a couple offstage as you make onstage."

"Of course I *like* Michael. He's a very nice guy and everything. But we're friends, that's all," Leah insisted. She looked out the window as the plane's engines roared. Then the plane started to move, and Leah found herself gripping the armrests of her seat.

"Don't be nervous, Leah. Here," Katrina said, reaching into her shoulder bag. She handed Leah a stick of gum. "Chew this. It'll keep your ears from plugging up while we take off."

Just then a stewardess approached the girls to check their seat belts and ask if they wanted headphones for the movie that was going to be shown later.

"What is the movie?" Leah asked.

"*White Nights,*" the stewardess replied. "I think it stars—"

"Baryshnikov!" Katrina and Leah cried in unison.

The stewardess laughed. "I take it you both want headphones, then?"

"Please," Katrina replied, reaching for the two cellophane-wrapped packages the stewardess was holding out to her.

"This is already fun," Leah said as the plane taxied down the runway. Then the plane started picking up speed, going faster and faster. Leah couldn't help feeling nervous, but chewing the spicy cinnamon gum did help distract her.

All at once the plane tilted up and, with a whoosh, they were in the air. As the plane rose higher and higher, Leah's fears vanished. Looking out the window, she saw San Francisco shrink beneath her and finally disappear. She felt like cheering. They were on their way!

"Would either of you girls care for something to drink?" the stewardess asked, returning with a big metal cart once the plane had leveled off.

Both Katrina and Leah asked for diet colas. Then they unwrapped their headphones and settled back to enjoy the movie.

"Isn't he gorgeous?" Katrina whispered with a sigh.

"Mmm," Leah mumbled. Then she added, "That reminds me, I hope Mrs. Hansom remembers to look after Misha and her kittens while I'm gone."

Katrina shook her head. "Leah, how can you be thinking about cats when *he's* up on the screen dancing. Ooh! Look at those eyes of his. I think I'm in love!"

Leah moaned. "Please! Don't mention that word!"

"You don't mean that!" Katrina exclaimed. "You haven't given up on love, have you?"

"Not completely," Leah admitted. The camera was moving in on Baryshnikov, and Leah couldn't stop her heart from beating faster. He was wonderful. Leah could hardly deny that.

"Wouldn't you give anything to actually meet him?" Katrina asked breathlessly.

"No," Leah assured her. "That would probably ruin everything. Right now all I'm interested in is love from afar—you know, the unrequited kind. I guess Misha is perfect for that."

"Which Misha are you talking about, Leah?" Katrina teased. "The cat or the danseur?"

Leah laughed. "Both!"

Chapter 2

"Katrina! Wake up!" Leah whispered loudly. Katrina had fallen asleep almost as soon as the van had picked them up at the airport in Burlington an hour earlier. "We're here!" she announced.

Michael leaned forward in his seat and rested his chin on the seat back between Leah and Katrina. "There's the Greenfield Inn," he said, pointing at a large white building. A small, casually dressed crowd was milling around on the wide front porch. "Doesn't that look just like the picture in my brochure?"

"It *is* the inn in the picture," Kenny pointed out sleepily.

Michael laughed. "Of course it is. But it looks just like the picture. Sometimes they airbrush those shots, you know, to make them look better than they really are. But this place looks great!"

"Boy, it's crowded here," Kenny commented.

"It's the height of the summer tourist season," Katrina reminded him, trying her best to fix her sleep-tousled hair. "I've been here during the off-season with my parents, and it's pretty quiet then."

As soon as Katrina had spoken, Leah realized they were about to leave the small town of Greenfield. Ahead of them Leah could just make out the dark outlines of the surrounding mountains.

"Are we close to Greenfield College yet?" Madame Preston asked the driver of the van, Mr. Parks.

"We sure are," the driver said to Madame, who was sitting up front with him. With that he turned into a tree-lined road that led to the campus. He pulled to a stop in front of a cluster of rectangular brick buildings. "Here we are," Mr. Parks said.

"These must be the dorms," Madame Preston observed, and the driver nodded. "You'll be staying here," Madame told the group as Mr. Parks got out of the van and started unloading their luggage. "I'm staying with Svetlana Lobinskya, who happens to be an old friend of mine, on the Ado estate."

"That's the artists' retreat we saw in Michael's brochure!" Leah exclaimed.

Madame chuckled. "That's right, Leah. And you will all be invited to have dinner with us as soon as Miss Lobinskya and I can decide on the best night. I'm anxious for you all to meet her. Summer Dance was her idea, you know."

After getting out of the van, Leah and the others gathered up their luggage. Madame called something to them out the open window as the van pulled away.

"What did Madame say?" Leah asked Michael as they started up the sidewalk toward the closest dorm, where registration was being held for the girls.

"She said our schedules would be with our registration material. She also said not to stay up too late." Michael laughed. "I think she was afraid we'd party all night if she didn't say something."

"Not tonight." Katrina yawned. "I'm too tired. I'm going right to bed."

"Me, too," Leah agreed as Michael opened the door for them. "We'll see you guys tomorrow!" Michael and Kenny headed for the boys' dorm next door, and she and Katrina slipped inside.

They found two packets with their names on them on a big table in the dorm lobby, under a banner that said Summer Dance Registration. There wasn't anyone at the desk, probably because it was so late.

It was a nice-looking room, Leah noted as she dug through the packet for her schedule of dance classes. There was a high-beamed cathedral ceiling and a huge fireplace made of different-sized stones covered one entire wall. The wood-framed furniture was covered with a green-and-blue-plaid material. All in all, it looked a lot like a ski chalet to Leah.

"Isn't this great?" Katrina said enthusiastically, joining Leah near the fireplace. "I bet it's wonderful in the winter when they have a huge fire blazing in here. Can't you imagine sitting here, sipping hot chocolate and watching it snow?"

Leah nodded. The surroundings were certainly different from the Victorian look of the San Francisco Ballet Academy. And it wasn't anything like the houses in her hometown, San Lorenzo, either. But she liked it.

"Let's go find our room," Katrina urged, heading for the big open stairway.

"Good idea. According to the schedule, we have class first thing tomorrow morning, even though it's Sunday," Leah pointed out.

The girls had just turned a corner on the third

floor when Leah saw a familiar-looking redheaded girl step into a room down the hall in front of them. "I can't believe it!" Leah cried out in surprise.

Katrina smiled. "Neither can I! This dorm is terrific."

"The dorm *is* great, but I wasn't talking about that. I think I just saw a girl I know from San Lorenzo," Leah said.

"Really? Who?" Katrina asked.

"Annie MacPhearson. We used to take dance classes together at Hannah Greene's. Maybe I've told you about her."

Katrina shook her head. "I don't remember. Is she our age?"

"She must be eighteen now," Leah said. "And the last I heard, she'd just been accepted into the corps of New York City Ballet."

"All right!" Katrina exclaimed, stopping suddenly. "Here's our room!"

Leah set down her duffel bag and opened the door, expecting to find something as charming and attractive as the main lobby. But as she flicked on the overhead light, her face fell. The off-white walls were bare, and the twin beds were unmade, giving an unfriendly look to the room. There was a long double window seat across from the beds, though, and a large window that gave them a perfect view of the campus. Leah also saw that there was a pile of linens, including blankets, sheets, pillows, and towels, folded into a neat pile on the window seat.

"It's kind of gloomy, isn't it?" Katrina commented. She set her bags down next to Leah's and turned slowly around, taking in the room that for the next two weeks would be their home.

"We can fix that," Leah said firmly. Crossing the room, she started separating the linens into two piles, one for herself and one for Katrina. "Tomorrow we'll go into Greenfield and buy a couple of posters for the walls."

Katrina nodded thoughtfully. "That's a good idea. But meanwhile, maybe it's good that it's kind of stark in here. Suddenly, I'm even more tired than I thought I was."

"Me, too," Leah agreed. Just touching the crisp cotton sheets made Leah eager to settle into them and go to sleep.

"Don't you want to go down the hall and see if the girl you saw really is your friend Annie?" Katrina asked as the girls finished making their beds.

Friend? Leah had never thought of Annie Mac-Phearson as her friend. In fact, back in San Lorenzo at Hannah Greene's School of Dance and Theater Arts, they had been rivals. But things were different now, Leah told herself. If Annie really was here, she had to be a festival participant, just like Leah. Maybe the gap that had always existed between the two girls was finally beginning to narrow.

"I'll go with you if you want me to," Katrina volunteered, obviously misinterpreting the cause of Leah's smile.

"It's pretty late," Leah pointed out. "I think I'll just wait until the morning to check it out. She'll still be here."

"Leah Stephenson! I don't believe it!" a familiar voice cried out just as Leah was about to take a tray in the breakfast line at the dining hall the next morning. Leah spun around and found herself staring right into Annie MacPhearson's turquoise blue eyes. Her wild red hair was neatly fixed in a tight bun.

"You must be Leah's friend Annie!" Katrina said excitedly. "Your room's right down the hall from ours in Baines."

"You're staying on the third floor of Baines? That's great!" Annie smiled as she threw her arms around Leah and gave her a friendly hug.

"Annie, this is my friend, Katrina Gray. We go to the San Francisco Ballet Academy together," Leah explained.

"Hi, Katrina." Then turning right back to Leah, Annie said, "I'd heard you were at the San Francisco Ballet Academy, Leah. It's supposed to be a terrific place to study. Do you like it?"

Leah nodded. "I love it."

"I love it, too," Katrina put in.

"Hey, are you girls going to eat or what?" a stocky boy in paint-spattered coveralls in line behind them demanded crossly. Leah decided he must be one of the art students she'd heard were also at the college now.

Annie walked beside Leah and Katrina as they started moving through the line again.

"Why don't you take a tray and join us, Annie?" Leah asked.

"I already ate. But I'll get another cup of tea and sit with you," Annie said. She pointed to a large round table in the middle of the circular dining hall. "I'll be over there."

"I'll bet you're thrilled to see someone you know from home," Katrina said when the girls stopped at the hot-drink table. "She seems really nice, and she's so beautiful, too."

Leah filled a cup with hot water and a tea bag and set it on her tray with her boiled egg and slice of unbuttered toast. "It is fun to see her," she admitted, a little surprised that what she said was true. She and Annie had never been close. But seeing her here made Leah feel differently about her. After all, they had grown up together.

"So, what do you hear from San Lorenzo, Leah?" Annie asked as soon as Leah and Katrina joined her. "Do you keep in touch with anyone back home?"

"I write to Chrissy," Leah told her.

"Chrissy Morley?" Annie asked. "Gosh, I haven't thought about her in ages. How is Chrissy? Does she still hate ballet class like she used to?"

Leah laughed. "Her mother finally let her quit last fall after I left for San Francisco. She insists that her ballet paid off, though, because she's a cheerleader now."

Annie shook her head. "Somehow I can't imagine Chrissy leading cheers. But I guess we've all changed. Right?"

Leah nodded as she took a bite of toast. "I'll say, and for the better, too. Chrissy even has a boyfriend. His name is Otto."

"Not Otto Rabinski?" Annie cried.

"Do you know him?" Leah asked.

"Well, sure. I used to have an incredible crush on his older brother, Karl." Annie's fair skin turned bright pink. "Seeing you sure brings back memories, Leah."

Leah glanced at Katrina and suddenly realized that all the reminiscing she and Annie were doing was leaving Katrina out. Katrina didn't really look upset, but Leah decided to move the conversation in a direction they'd all enjoy.

"And what about you, Annie?" Leah asked. She carefully sipped the hot tea. "I hear you're a member of City Ballet now. Living in New York must agree with you."

"I do love New York," Annie confirmed. "It's noisy and crowded, but it's definitely the most exciting city on earth. You should visit me sometime, both of you."

"Wouldn't that be fun, Leah?" Katrina exclaimed.

Leah nodded. "It would be great. You should visit us in San Francisco."

"Oh, oh," Annie said, pointing up at the wall clock over the outside door. "We better head out. We don't want to be late for class."

"Do you know who's leading class this morning, Annie?" Katrina asked after the girls had bused their dishes. As they stepped outside, Leah slipped off her boldly striped cotton sweater and tied it loosely around her neck.

"Bryce Coleman," Annie answered. "He's one of our big-name teachers at City Ballet. You'll love him. I've taken class from him before."

"It must be wonderful to be in New York," Katrina said with a sigh. "That's really where I wanted to study, but my parents didn't want me living there." Katrina shook her head. "Sometimes my parents don't make a lot of sense."

Annie nodded sympathetically. "I could say the same thing about my own parents, especially my mother."

"Is your mother still living with you in New York?" Leah asked as the girls started up the stairs of the campus recital hall. She remembered

Annie's mother as being the most overbearing stage mother she had ever met.

"No, she went home when she realized there wasn't much for her to do in New York while I was dancing. Finally!" Annie said, grinning.

Leah decided Annie had every right to be glad her mother had gone back to California. Pushy mothers like Annie's could drive a person crazy. Then Leah smiled. Maybe it was Annie's mother that had made her so competitive in the past. Maybe now that her mother was gone, Annie was free to be herself. Whatever the reason, she seemed so much nicer now. Leah was sure she and Annie could be friends. It was a nice feeling.

"Very nice," Bryce Coleman said, pausing to stand next to Leah. Leah detected a sparkle in his eyes as he watched her execute a full plié, moving her arms from fifth to first position.

Madame Preston had frequently complimented Leah on the grace of her arm movements. Once Madame had even compared Leah's port de bras to Pavlova's. But having the dashing, dark-haired danseur compliment her, especially while she was standing at the barre with famous dancers like Brent Bartholomew and Christina DeWitt, made Leah flush with pride.

Bryce Coleman's compliments helped confirm for Leah that she'd finally caught up with the other girls after her injury. After all, he hadn't seen Leah dance before her injury, nor did he care about making an extra effort to encourage Leah because of that injury, as Leah had suspected some of the SFBA teachers of doing.

When Bryce moved on, Leah focused her attention on Annie, who was a couple of dancers in front of her at the barre. Annie was more graceful than ever, and it made Leah glad that they both seemed to have made a lot of progress since their days at Hannah Greene's.

When their barre work was over, Leah got her bag and began changing into her toe shoes for the centre work that was to follow. She was carefully padding her big toe with lamb's wool when Elena Moraldi, an Italian ballerina currently guesting with the American Ballet Theatre, sat down next to her to put on her own shoes.

"Where have you been training, my dear?" Miss Moraldi asked Leah pleasantly. "Your port de bras is superb."

"I'm a student at the San Francisco Ballet Academy," Leah replied shyly, more than a little surprised that Miss Moraldi would even speak to her, much less pay her a compliment.

Miss Moraldi nodded. "Alicia Preston is your teacher, then, no?" Leah nodded, and Miss Moraldi smiled. "You are very lucky, my dear. Madame Preston is the perfect teacher for a dancer with your gifts."

Leah returned the older woman's smile. "Thank you," she said sincerely, feeling her cheeks blush.

Later, in the large backstage dressing room, Leah searched for Annie and Katrina. She especially wanted to share Miss Moraldi's kind remarks with them.

"Wasn't that a terrific class?" Leah asked when she finally spotted Katrina and Annie at the long dressing room mirror fixing their hair.

"It sure was," Katrina agreed. "Bryce Coleman actually called my fouettés brilliant! Remember when I couldn't do more than a few of them at a time?"

Leah laughed as she pulled the elastic out of her hair. "That was a long time ago."

"Not that long ago," Katrina insisted. "Anyway, I think he's nice."

"I do, too," Leah agreed. "He said some nice things to me, too. And you know who else said something to me?"

"Who?" Katrina demanded.

"Elena Moraldi!" Leah cried. Then she quickly looked around to make sure the ballerina wasn't within hearing distance. When Annie didn't say anything, Leah worried that she wasn't as happy about the first class as she and Katrina were.

"I watched you a little, Annie. You look great," Leah complimented her, smiling at Annie's reflection in the dressing room mirror. Annie didn't meet Leah's gaze.

"I like being told how well I'm doing as much as you do, Leah. But sometimes corrections mean more," Annie said. She turned around and dropped her brush into her big white carryall.

Surprised more by the tone of Annie's voice than by what she'd just said, Leah turned to see if Katrina might have noticed how critical Annie sounded. But Katrina was bent over her own dance bag, searching for something. Deciding she was making something out of nothing, Leah shrugged. Maybe Annie had been irritated by Leah's relating the compliments she'd received. Or maybe she was just tired from the night before. Well, whatever it was, Leah told herself, it was probably no big deal.

Chapter 3

Leah was finishing a letter to Kay so she could mail it when she and Katrina went into town to buy some posters, when there was a knock at the door.

"Katrina! Leah!" Annie called through the closed door. "Can I come in?"

"Sure. Come on in," Katrina called back. She tossed down the book she'd been reading and jumped to her feet.

"I have some exciting news!" Annie announced as soon as she walked through the door. Annie was wearing her curly red hair in a braid. Her black parachute pants and sleeveless green top, coupled with large gold-hoop earrings, gave her a sophisticated look that Leah really liked. "I asked around and found out there's a place in town that actually rents bicycles! How about it? We could explore Greenfield this afternoon."

"That would be fun, wouldn't it, Katrina?" Leah said. Whatever had been bothering Annie after their class with Bryce Coleman earlier that day didn't seem to be bothering her now. She was as friendly as she'd been at breakfast, and Leah was glad. "I'd kind of like to ride out to Ado, you know, that artists' retreat. Madame Preston is

22

staying there. Maybe we'll even run into her," Leah mused. She smiled at Annie.

Katrina nodded. "I wouldn't mind taking a bike ride. We can always get those posters we talked about some other time."

"All right, then," Annie said enthusiastically. "Greenfield, here we come!"

The walk to town from the campus was about the same distance that Leah traveled to get from her boardinghouse in San Francisco to the San Francisco Ballet Academy, often several times a day. As they walked, Annie told Katrina and Leah what it was like living with four other girls in a one-bedroom apartment in Manhattan.

"Of course no one cleans up the kitchen. It's always dirty, but no one will admit to being the one to use it last. Then, every so often, Alysse Daniels's mother takes the train in from New Jersey and cleans up everything." Annie laughed. "She always comes when no one is around and leaves before anyone gets back, you know, like an elf or something. It really bugs Alysse, but the rest of us love it."

"It sounds like fun," Katrina said.

Annie shrugged. "It is, but sometimes sharing one bathroom, one bedroom, and one kitchen with that many other girls can get on your nerves."

"I bet," Leah sympathized. "Sometimes Mrs. Hanson's gets a little hairy, and that's a huge old house. I can't imagine being cooped up in a little apartment with that many people."

"It's not that bad," Annie assured her. Then her face brightened as she pointed across the street. "There's the rental place!"

Annie led the way to a small shop with a sign

above the door that said Bagley's Bicycles. Pulling open the door, Annie waited for Leah and Katrina to enter, then followed them inside.

"Oh, Leah!" Katrina cried right away. "Look at that. A bicycle built for two!"

Leah was about to say that she didn't think the heavy-looking double bicycle would be very practical, with all the long, steep hills around Greenfield, when Annie said, "Let's rent that one for sure. We can take turns on it."

"You two can rent it," Leah said good-naturedly. "I'll just rent a regular bicycle built for one."

"Can I help you girls?" a man asked, coming out of a back room. His hands were covered with black grease, which he attempted to rub off on his already-stained apron.

Annie strolled over to the counter. "We'd like to rent that bicycle and one other one for the afternoon," she said. "What are your rates?"

"Five dollars an hour for the tandem. Three for a regular touring bike," the man replied briskly.

"That sounds reasonable. We'll want them for at least two hours, don't you think?" Annie asked, turning to Leah and Katrina.

Katrina nodded. "At least."

"I'll need a twenty-five-dollar cash deposit for each bike, then. We'll settle up when you get back," the man told them. Leah heard Katrina gasp. She knew that even if she and Katrina pooled their money, they couldn't come up with even half of what the man was asking for as a deposit.

"Can I leave this with you instead?" Annie asked. She reached into the pocket of her parachute pants and produced a gold-trimmed credit card.

The man took the card and examined it closely. "This yours?" he asked, sounding suspicious.

"Yes," Annie replied, standing tall. "I'm Annie MacPhearson."

Suddenly the man's weathered face broke into a smile. "Say, you're one of the ballerinas that's here for the dance festival, aren't you?"

Annie returned his smile as she nodded her head. "I'm with the New York City Ballet," she told him.

He grinned, tapping the edge of the card on the counter in front of him. "My wife is a big ballet fan. She might have been a ballerina herself if she hadn't married me."

Leah cringed. It was nice that Annie had a credit card and everything, but she was really showing off, and it made Leah uncomfortable.

Once the girls were out on the sidewalk with their bikes, Katrina said, "Aren't Vermonters great? He was so friendly and sincere. Sometimes I miss that in San Francisco."

"Katrina, people are friendly in San Francisco, too," Leah protested.

"I didn't mean that they weren't," Katrina said. "It's just that San Francisco is a big city. Life is slower and easier here in Vermont."

"I know what you mean, Katrina," Annie told her, smiling. "And I agree with you. I really liked that man. Besides, he was a fan."

Leah had to bite her tongue to keep from pointing out that Annie had deceived the man into thinking she was a principal dancer or at least a soloist with City Ballet, instead of merely a member of the corps. But then, Leah reminded herself, Annie was still a step ahead of her. Leah wasn't even in the corps yet. She decided to keep her opinion to herself, at least for the time being.

Katrina and Annie got on the tandem and led the way through the center of town. Leah could tell they were discussing something, but she couldn't make out exactly what. They motioned to Leah to turn at the next corner. Leah did and found herself coasting down a steep hill toward a lovely park. The girls came to a stop just inside the stone arch that marked the park's entrance. Leah pulled up alongside them.

"This is Rose Park," Katrina informed Leah. "There's a beautiful little man-made lake in the center of the park, where they rent rowboats in the evenings and on weekends during the summer."

"Let's ride to the lake," Annie said. "I heard from someone that there's a band shell near the lake, where they sometimes have concerts."

"Are you sure you don't want to try this bike out, Leah?" Katrina asked before getting back on the tandem behind Annie. "It's lots of fun."

Leah shook her head. "You go ahead, Katrina, but thanks. It's been a while since I've been bike riding. I think I'm better off riding alone."

When they found the band shell, Annie insisted on going up on the little wooden stage. "The best part of Summer Dance is that we'll be performing outside on Fridays and Saturdays, since the Performing Arts Center is an open-air theater." Then, kicking off her white sneakers, Annie began to dance around the stage in her bare feet.

"She's going to get a sliver in her foot," Leah mumbled to herself. Annie seemed to be showing off again, and for some reason it irritated Leah.

"Did you say something, Leah?" Katrina asked, but Leah shook her head.

Finally Annie picked up her shoes and joined them. "It's so beautiful here," she said with a sigh. "New York is exciting, but after a while the dirt and the noise get to you. I guess that's why so many New Yorkers come up here to—" But instead of finishing her sentence, Annie rushed right past Leah and Katrina toward a large bulletin board covered with notices.

"Oh, look!" she cried excitedly. "There's going to be a dance here Friday night. We've just got to come back for it!"

"But we'll be performing Friday night," Leah pointed out.

"Only until ten o'clock. It says here that the dance goes on until midnight," Annie countered.

"It sounds like fun," Katrina said.

"Then it's settled. Now all we need are three dates." Annie sat down on the whitewashed steps of the band shell to put her shoes back on.

"There are two boys here from our academy," Katrina said eagerly. "I'm sure Michael and Kenny would think an open-air dance was great. Don't you think so, Leah?"

Leah chuckled. "Especially Michael."

"Michael?" Annie repeated.

"Michael Litvak," Katrina told her. "He's Leah's pas de deux partner."

"He's not the only guy I dance with," Leah said, "but he is the guy I'm going to be working with here."

"And in the fall," Katrina reminded her.

"Two boys and three girls," Annie said thoughtfully. "There aren't ever enough boys to go around, are there?" Then she smiled. "I know! I'll ask Bryce Coleman to come, too. So, where to now?" Annie asked. "Ado?"

"Sure," Katrina said. "Let's go."

The ride out to Ado was a longer one than Leah had anticipated, and the road was hilly. Leah felt like turning back a couple of times, but neither Annie nor Katrina showed any signs of tiring, so she kept going.

"Here we are," Katrina announced as Leah pulled up alongside the tandem.

"Finally," Leah said with a groan. Pulling an elastic out of the pocket of her high-waisted suspender pants, she pulled her thick blond hair back into a ponytail, noting as she did that the back of her neck was damp with perspiration. Overdoing it on the bikes probably wasn't a smart thing for dancers to do, she thought.

"You aren't out of shape, are you, Leah?" Annie asked.

Before Leah could respond, Katrina said, "Leah was injured last winter. It was pretty serious, too. She had to wear a cast and everything."

"I'm totally recovered from that," Leah quickly insisted.

"It sounds like you were lucky," Annie said.

"I was," Leah agreed. "Anyway, I think we ought to get moving if we're going to ride around the estate. We still have to get back to town, don't forget." With that, Leah pushed off. A little angry at what she considered Katrina's thoughtless reference to her injury, Leah sped down the main road into the estate. Katrina ought to know that Leah just wanted to put her injury behind her. Now she was afraid everyone at Summer Dance was going to find out from Annie that she'd been seriously injured just a short time ago. When the paved road ended and three narrow dirt roads began, Leah had to stop and wait for the others.

"That one goes to the main house," Katrina said, pointing to the middle road as the tandem cruised up next to Leah and came to a stop. "The road on the left goes to the cottages, and the one on the right goes to the public sculpture gardens. The cottages and the main house aren't open to the public," Katrina added.

"But you know Madame Preston well enough to drop in on her, don't you?" Annie asked.

"What do you think, Leah?" Katrina asked, turning toward Leah. They were Madame Preston's students, but neither girl could really say they knew the SFBA director well enough to drop in on her.

"I don't think it would be a good idea," Leah said honestly. "Madame might not be there, and Miss Lobinskya doesn't even know us."

"Madame Preston is staying with Svetlana Lobinskya?" Annie exclaimed. "That's great! I'd really like to meet Miss Lobinskya. She's one of the grandes dames of ballet, you know."

"Let's go to the sculpture gardens for now," Katrina suggested. Both Annie and Leah agreed, and the girls started riding again.

At the end of the road was a small parking area, complete with a bike rack. The girls parked their bikes and started down the gravel path that was lined with brightly colored flowers. They had just stopped in front of the first sculpture to admire it when someone called to Katrina and Leah. It was Madame Preston!

"What a pleasant surprise to find you girls here. Miss Lobinskya and I were just discussing the best time to have you to dinner," Madame said. Then she smiled at Annie. "And who have we here?"

But before Leah could say anything, Annie introduced herself. "My name is Annie MacPhearson, Madame Preston. Leah and I used to take ballet together back in San Lorenzo."

"Then you were a student of Hannah Greene's," Madame said. "Miss Greene and I go way back, you know. Now wait right here, you three. There is someone I want you to meet. Svetlana, dear, where have you gone off to?" Madame asked, looking around.

Suddenly an old but beautifully angular face appeared above the tallest flowers. Svetlana Lobinskya's once-dark hair was now as white as snow. She still wore it pulled back in a tight bun that emphasized her long, slender neck. "Why, Alicia, are these girls your students?" Miss Lobinskya inquired with a British accent. "You must be Leah Stephenson," she remarked, smiling at Leah. "Madame has described you so thoroughly that I would know you anywhere, Leah. And you, of course, are Katrina Gray."

Madame Preston beamed proudly. "Katrina was the recipient of our Louise Adams Scholarship. She proved that we chose wisely by the way she handled the difficult dual role of Odette-Odile in our student performance of *Swan Lake.*"

Miss Lobinskya smiled at Katrina. "Quite an honor for one so young. But then, ballet is an old art for young people to practice, isn't it, Alicia, my dear?"

"Yes, yes it is." Madame Preston nodded.

"And who are you, love?" Miss Lobinskya asked, stepping carefully through the flower bed to join the others.

"I'm Annie MacPhearson, Miss Lobinskya. I'm in the corps of City Ballet. Leah and I took ballet lessons together when we were children."

Miss Lobinskya looked from Annie to Leah and back again, her dark eyes glowing. "Old friendships are precious. You girls should nurture this. One day you'll be old, like Madame Preston and me. Then you will be glad to have someone to share your memories with, someone who understands."

Madame Preston shook her head. "We are not so very old, Svetlana."

Miss Lobinskya chuckled. "In the dance world one is old all too soon. But enough of that kind of talk. Our friends are young, and that's what's important. We are handing the flame to them, and they are carrying on the traditions. Madame tells me you girls want to have dinner with us?"

"Oh, yes," Katrina said. "That would be wonderful, wouldn't it, Leah?"

"Tuesday is the evening we decided on, isn't it, Alicia?" Miss Lobinskya asked.

Madame nodded. "And please bring Annie with you, Leah. Svetlana is right about old friendships. They're precious."

Leah stole a glance at Annie. There wasn't an *old* friendship between them, but she wondered if they could start one now.

"Oh, be sure to invite Kenny and Michael," Madame Preston added. Then Madame and Miss Lobinskya retreated down the garden path in the direction of the artists' cottages.

"They're both wonderful," Annie said with an admiring sigh once the older women had disappeared into the depths of the sculpture garden. "I can't wait to spend an evening with them and to meet Kenny and Michael, too."

"Then you're going to come!" Katrina exclaimed. "I'm glad, aren't you, Leah?"

Leah nodded, but the truth was, she wasn't sure how happy she really was. Leah couldn't help wondering where all Annie's New York friends were.

Chapter 4

Standing in front of the large mirror in the hallway of the dorm, Leah admired her new radiant blue bubble dress, with its wisp of fuschia tulle fluttering below the skirt. It was hard to believe it was Tuesday evening already and time for the dinner party at Miss Lobinskya's. It seemed as though Leah's worries about spending too much time with Annie had been groundless. Both Annie and Leah had been too busy with classes and rehearsals to spend much time together since their Sunday afternoon bike ride.

Suddenly Katrina's reflection joined Leah's in the large mirror. "Wow, that dress is great! It's new, isn't it?"

Leah nodded. "Chrissy helped me pick it out last time I was home." She pulled at the skirt, making it balloon some more. "You don't think it's too much for tonight, do you?"

"Oh, no," Katrina assured her. "It's perfect on you, Leah."

Leah beamed. "Thanks, Katrina." Then, shifting her gaze, Leah saw that Katrina had on a peasant blouse and a cotton skirt with a pattern of purple and blue wildflowers. It was an outfit Leah had seen before, but Katrina's hairstyle was new, which gave her a whole new look that was decidedly soft and romantic. She'd twisted and braided her long, wavy hair into a cascade of curls that softly framed her pretty brown eyes.

"I really like your hair," Leah told her. Then she gathered up a handful of her blond hair, trying to decide how to wear it that evening. "I guess I don't have time to do anything special with mine." She dropped her hair so that it fell about her neck and shoulders.

"Your hair always looks good, Leah," Katrina assured her as a third figure joined theirs in the mirror.

"I think so, too, Leah. It's so perfectly straight," Annie said. She looked stunning in a white minidress that buttoned snugly up the front. Her thick hair cascaded in crimped curls about her bare shoulders.

Leah was still trying to decide whether Annie had just complimented or insulted her, when Katrina pointed at her watch. "We should get going. Madame said she was sending a car around for us."

"Where are the boys? Aren't they going with us?" Annie asked.

"They had a special men's class that started late," Leah told her, leading them down the hallway to the stairs. "They're going to meet us there."

Katrina laughed. "I hope they don't know yet Miss Lobinskya is really English and not Russian. I want to see their expressions when they hear her talk. It blew me away."

"I haven't told them," Leah assured her.

"You two didn't know before you met her?" Annie sounded surprised. "I thought everyone did! Anyway, in her day it was more fashionable in the ballet world to be Russian. I think I read somewhere that she had a perfectly awful name for a ballerina, so she had to change it anyway."

"I wonder what her name was?" Katrina mused. She opened the door of the dorm for the other two girls. It was still bright and sunny out. The college campus was alive with shouts and laughter, and a Frisbee sailed past them into someone's arms.

"I bet that's the car that's picking us up." Annie nodded toward the curb, where a sleek black car was parked, its engine idling. Leah smiled. She felt like a princess about to step into her carriage, to be whisked away to an enchanted ball!

"Come in, come in!" Miss Lobinskya greeted them warmly. "You girls look so lovely," she said, leading them into her cozy living room. "As you can see, this is a small cottage, but it's perfect for me."

Madame appeared at the other end of the living room. She was wearing an apron over her crisp white slacks and had clearly been busy in the kitchen. "I have dinner under control," Madame informed them. "You girls must get Svetlana to tell you about her career while I finish up in here. I'm sure her stories will prove inspiring."

"Oh, Alicia! You're embarrassing me!" Miss Lobinskya declared.

"You must know the girls haven't dressed up as they have to impress *me*," Madame countered, her usually stern face lit by a smile. "Now sit down, all of you. The boys will be here shortly, and they'll want to eat." With that, Madame turned on her heels and retreated into the kitchen.

"Actually," Miss Lobinskya began as she sat down and urged the others to do so with a graceful motion of her long, slender hand, "I'm the one who's eager to hear about you. I want to know what the Bay Area Ballet is like these days and also which dancers are up-and-coming at City Ballet. I have guested with both these companies but *so* long ago." Her dark eyes sparkled.

"We'll answer all of your questions," Annie promised. "But first tell us about changing your name." She looked at Katrina and winked.

Miss Lobinskya threw back her head and laughed. "Yes, that *is* a good story. You see, not knowing that I was destined to become a top ballerina, my parents named me Mabel. Mabel Alice Terwilliger, to be exact." Miss Lobinskya paused to shake her head. "It wasn't an awful name, but I felt it lacked the dignity I needed back then. So, Nicholas Weatherby—"

"*The* Nicholas Weatherby?" Annie interrupted to ask.

The corners of Miss Lobinskya's mouth turned up in a smile, but her eyes looked sad. "Nicky and I were students together a long time ago. Anyway, it was Nick who came up with my name, Svetlana Lobinskya. And it was a smashing good idea, too. I often think if I'd stayed Mabel Terwilliger, I never would have made it out of the corps."

"Do you have any pictures?" Katrina asked.

"Oh, yes!" Annie seconded. "Do you have pictures of Nicholas Weatherby when he was young?"

Miss Lobinskya pretended to look hurt. "Are you more interested in Nicky than you are in me, then?"

Annie's fair skin turned almost as red as her hair. "No, of course not," she protested. "It's just that there are so few pictures of him available. My mother used to talk about seeing him dance when she was a girl. The regional company he was with in the fifties often danced at small, out-of-the-way places like San Lorenzo, California —my hometown. If it wasn't for Nicholas Weatherby, my mother might never have decided to encourage me to dance, the way she did."

Miss Lobinskya nodded. "I understand, Annie. He's an inspiring person." She got up and began walking across the room in the direction of a large antique buffet.

"He's still alive, isn't he?" Annie called after her.

Miss Lobinskya opened the middle drawer in the chest and pulled out several leather-bound photo albums. Then she turned back toward the girls.

"Nicky is quite healthy. We haven't seen much of each other lately, but I follow his comings and goings, and he does the same. We even correspond now and again."

The girls were poring over the picture albums with the retired ballerina when the door knocker sounded. "That must be your mates," Miss Lobinskya said.

Katrina stood up. "I'll let them in."

When Katrina came back with Kenny and Michael in tow, she introduced them to Miss Lobinskya and then to Annie.

Kenny looked as cute as ever, Leah noted, with his dark, spiky hair and his twinkling eyes. But Michael looked different to her somehow. He'd combed his hair back from his face in a different way that showed off the strong cut of his jaw. Meanwhile, the longer hair around the back of his neck seemed to be still a little damp from the shower, and it had curled slightly just behind his ears. The gawky look that Leah had come to associate with Michael was definitely gone. In fact, he looked totally self-assured in his dark trousers and the checked blazer he'd worn over an oxford button-down shirt. Self-assured and handsome.

"Hi, guys," Leah said, pleased when Michael came to sit next to her on the couch. "You're just in time to see some of Miss Lobinskya's pictures."

"Nice dress," Michael said softly, smiling at Leah.

"Thank you," Leah said. She felt herself blush.

"So, what have we missed?" Kenny asked. He pulled a smaller chair up to join the group and was leaning forward, looking at the photo album expectantly. Leah was just about to catch the boys up on their conversation when Madame appeared to announce dinner.

Leah started to get up, prepared to walk into the other room with Michael. But before she could even move, Annie was standing next to him.

"Leah has told me so much about you, Michael," Annie said, laying her hand on his arm. Michael returned Annie's smile and the two of them started toward the dining room.

"She has?" Michael asked. He sounded both surprised and pleased.

Annie nodded. "I couldn't wait to meet you." Leah could tell Michael was flattered. She wasn't at all surprised when they got to the dining room and Annie took the place next to Michael. Leah had no choice but to sit across from them, on the other side of Kenny.

"You see, girls?" Madame said once everyone was seated, the two older women at either end of the table. "My sister is not the only cook in the family." Then Madame explained, "Leah has a room in my sister's boardinghouse."

"I remember when I stayed with the Hansons last time I guested with the Bay Area Ballet for a season. I won't even tell you children how long ago that was, either. Anyway, you're a lucky girl, Leah. Mrs. Hanson is a very warm woman indeed," Miss Lobinskya said.

Leah smiled politely and nodded. But her mind wasn't on Mrs. Hanson at the moment. It was on Michael and Annie, sitting side by side, staring dreamily into each other's eyes. They were talking, but so softly that Leah couldn't hear what they were saying.

"How do you like living in San Francisco, Michael?" Leah heard Annie ask when the rest of the table quieted down for a moment.

Michael shrugged. "There are things I like and things I don't like." Then he looked nervously at Madame.

Madame laughed. "Don't worry, Michael. There are a few things I don't like about San Francisco myself."

"Annie lives in New York City," Katrina told the two boys. "She's already a member of City Ballet."

"Really?" Michael said. Leah thought she saw a new level of admiration for Annie in his eyes. "That's fabulous. Congratulations."

"I moved to New York when I was fourteen so I

could be an apprentice with the New York City Ballet," Annie told him. "It's the best thing I've ever done. California is okay, but I really love New York."

Michael nodded. "I think the East Coast is the place to be, too. Certainly for dance, and probably for everything else as well."

"How can you say that, Michael? There's wonderful ballet on the West Coast." Leah felt she should defend California, considering she'd lived there all her life.

"Now, Leah," Madame Preston said soothingly. "Everyone is entitled to an opinion."

Miss Lobinskya nodded. "In my day Russia was the place to be, or at least, to be *from.* Now it is New York, I suppose. Leah, Madame Preston tells me you were the recipient of The Golden Gate Award last fall. I think I have also seen photos of you in *FootNotes.* Have you thought at all about which company you will eventually join?"

"I just hope some company will want me," Leah answered truthfully.

"But you are taken with the West Coast, right? Does that mean you'll be looking for a company there?" Miss Lobinskya pressed.

"I do love California. I love the Bay Area Ballet, too," Leah admitted. "Of course dancing on the War Memorial Opera House stage would be a dream come true. But I'm not sure right now what I'll do."

"I agree with Leah. There are so many factors, factors that are always changing, too, factors that can change the flavor of a company overnight and change one's desire to be part of that company," Annie said, reaching for the bread basket at the same time Michael did. Their fingers brushed, and Leah saw them exchange an intense look.

Katrina nodded. "Right now I think I'd like to be part of a more classically oriented company, you know, one that does full-length ballets."

"The size of the danseurs in a company is important, too. Taller men must dance with taller women, and vice versa," Annie said. "A dancer wants to look her best, of course, and the man she is dancing with is a crucial part of how she looks."

Miss Lobinskya nodded. "Yes, as Balanchine used to say, 'Dance is woman.' But the importance of the danseur shouldn't be underestimated."

Leah glanced at Michael, hoping to catch his eye. The day before, they had begun learning the third act pas de deux from *Coppélia* in the partnering workshop Madame was teaching. She thought they were doing well with it. For the first time she wondered if he felt the same way.

But Michael wasn't looking in Leah's direction. He was staring intently at Annie instead. As Leah watched, Annie slowly raised her turquoise blue eyes until they met Michael's dark brown ones. Then Annie smiled shyly.

"So you think having the right partner is very important then, Miss Lobinskaya?" Annie asked, all the while looking at Michael.

Miss Lobinskya nodded. "It is everything," she agreed.

After slipping into her nightie, Leah took her brush over to the window seat to brush out her long blond hair.

"Did you see the way Michael was looking at

Annie tonight?" Katrina chuckled slightly as she sat down on the other end of the window seat.

"I sure did," Leah muttered, beginning to brush her hair more vigorously. "And I don't blame him, either. She was practically throwing herself at him."

"I guess I didn't see that," Katrina said. "She did seem interested in him, though. Personally, I'm glad for Michael."

"I'm not." Leah set down her brush and leaned back to look out the window at the campus. The cool night air was drifting in, along with the sounds of a chorus of crickets.

"But I thought Annie was your friend, Leah." Katrina looked questioningly at Leah. "I thought Michael was, too."

"Michael and I are friends. But Annie and I never were," Leah admitted. "We were serious rivals back in San Lorenzo. At first I thought things could be different. I thought Annie had changed. But I'm not so sure anymore."

"That doesn't make any sense," Katrina protested. "She's been really friendly to both of us, especially you. Besides, she's already a member of an important ballet company. Why would she feel competitive with us?"

Leah hopped off the window seat and crossed the long, narrow room to her bed. "Some people are just like that, Katrina. In fact, I don't think Annie is interested in Michael at all. She's just trying to make a point with him because she knows we're partners here at Summer Dance. She's flirting with him to show me up."

"Oh, Leah. You're imagining things," Katrina said. She smiled. "I think you're the one who's competitive, and you're just afraid to admit it.

Maybe you have a crush on Michael after all," Katrina teased. "Maybe that's what's really bothering you."

Leah shook her head adamantly. "I'm not jealous! Sometimes you can be so blind, Katrina! I suppose you didn't see the way Annie was batting her eyelashes at Michael on the walk back, when she invited him to go to that dance in Rose Park Friday night."

"Maybe I didn't see that," Katrina confessed. "But I did see the way Michael was looking at her, and she didn't have to do much to get his attention. She's incredibly pretty. Just because she was nice to him doesn't mean she was flirting with him. And even if she was, why do you care? Would you have been happier if she'd ignored Michael and made him miserable?"

"Maybe," Leah told her as she pulled back her covers. Then she paused before getting into bed. "You know, it really hurts to have you side against me, Katrina. I thought we were friends."

"Of course we're friends! But I like Annie, too. Anyway, I'm not taking sides because I don't think there are any sides to take." Katrina walked over to her own bed and sat down. "Maybe you're the one who feels competitive with Annie, Leah. Maybe that's why a few little things she's said or done are suddenly bothering you so much. Have you stopped to consider that?"

Leah sighed. It was all so confusing. She just wanted to enjoy her stay in Vermont. If only Annie hadn't shown up, she would be doing that instead of arguing with Katrina.

"Maybe things will seem better to you in the

morning," Katrina suggested as she turned off the light over her bed. "Well, good night."

"Good night," Leah said glumly as she turned off her own light.

Chapter 5

"I'll let you kids out here," Bryce Coleman said. He stopped his car near the entrance of Rose Park and waited for Leah and the others to get out.

"Shall we wait for you?" Leah asked.

Bryce shook his head. "No, I'll catch up with you later. Finding a parking place might take a while."

As the group started up the path to the band shell, Leah found it hard to believe it was Friday and the end of the first week of Summer Dance already. Their first performance had gone extremely well, Leah thought, and she was in the mood to celebrate. She was especially pleased that Annie had talked Bryce into coming to the dance with them. Bryce reminded Leah of her friend Andrei Levintoff, and she really enjoyed being around him.

Leah had had only one small part in the corps in one ballet that night, but she was happy anyway. She and Michael had been working on the pas de deux from *Coppélia,* and they seemed to be dancing even better together in Madame's workshop than they had been back in San Francisco. Madame not only complimented them on their adagio but continually asked them to demonstrate for the other couples as well.

Leah was just about to say something to Michael about their class earlier that day when she noticed Annie slip her arm through Michael's. When Michael turned his head and smiled at Annie, Leah saw a tender look in his dark eyes. She'd seen that look before, she realized with a jolt. Michael used to look at her that way.

As they got closer to the center of the park, she heard a U2 song that she recognized as the one her best friend Chrissy had said was the favorite at San Lorenzo High. "All right!" Kenny whooped. "Want to dance, Katrina?"

Katrina giggled. "I'm not sure I remember how."

"It's easy." Kenny took her hand and pulled her into the crowd. "Just pretend you're working on one of Kay's ballets."

Leah laughed as Kenny and Katrina headed out onto the dance floor. They looked great dancing together. She turned to say something about it to Michael, but she discovered he wasn't standing next to her anymore. Obviously Michael and Annie had slipped away without telling her. Then she saw them dancing under some colored lanterns that had been swung across the lawn. They were dancing the same way that Kenny and Katrina were, but instead of looking light and funny, Annie and Michael seemed intense. In fact, they looked as if they were made to dance together. Everything about them was right, from their contrasting coloring to their complementary heights and physiques. Leah knew in her heart that she and Michael had never looked as good together as Annie and Michael did.

Suddenly Leah wished she hadn't come to the dance in the first place. She didn't know anyone there at all. She looked around for Bryce but couldn't see him. Slowly she began backing into the shadows, hoping no one would notice her slip away.

"Leah!"

Leah jumped at the sound of her name and spun around. It was Bryce.

"I finally found you. I thought I was going to be stuck here alone." He surveyed the crowd for a moment. "I don't see anyone else here from Summer Dance. Do you?" he asked.

Leah shook her head. "No. Just our group."

"Well, never mind. It doesn't matter. Let's dance." He indicated the gyrating crowd with a toss of his head. Someone had changed the disc, and now a Bruce Springsteen song was playing.

"Sure," Leah agreed. Anything would be better than standing around watching Annie flirt with Michael. "Let's go!"

Bryce smiled as he started to move. "This is a great way to blow off steam." One song ended and another began, but the fast beat stayed the same.

"I need to take a break," Bryce said after the third song. He pulled a handkerchief out of his back pocket and mopped his forehead with it. "I'm not as young as I used to be. How about something to drink?"

Leah nodded, planning to go with him. But she lost him as they tried to make their way through the crowd.

Feeling even more forlorn than she had earlier, Leah wandered over to the band shell, where a couple of guys were sitting at a table. They had several boxes of compact discs in front of them, and they seemed to be in an argument of sorts over what to play next.

"Would you like to dance, Leah?" Kenny asked, coming up beside her.

Leah smiled. "That's okay," she said. "You don't need to play big brother, Kenny. Go on and dance with Katrina. You guys are great together."

Kenny hesitated. "Are you sure?" he asked, but Leah sensed he'd rather be dancing with Katrina. "I really like dancing with you, Leah. You know that."

"I know," Leah assured him. "But Katrina's your Summer Dance partner. It's good for you two to become familiar with each other."

"I talked to Bryce a few minutes ago. He suggested we meet by the park entrance at midnight. Are you sure you're all right?" Kenny asked one last time. When Leah nodded, Kenny hurried back to Katrina.

As soon as she was alone again, Leah decided to walk over to the rose gardens. The moon was nearly full, and it was flooding the park with light.

She had almost reached the shore of the small lake when she saw the silhouette of two people kissing near the beached rowboats in front of her. She stopped walking. The scene was so romantic, and she didn't want to disturb them.

After a few moments Leah began to feel as though she was spying on the pair. Carefully she crept backward, hoping to sneak away unnoticed.

Suddenly the couple pulled apart. "Leah!" a male voice called out to her. "Is that you?"

It was Michael! He'd been kissing Annie!

Without taking time to answer, Leah turned and ran away.

"I don't think they're coming," Bryce said, looking at his wristwatch impatiently. "It's already twenty past twelve. I'm afraid we'll have to leave now." He took a step toward his car and opened the back door. Looking up at Leah, he asked, "Coming?"

"Let's go," Kenny said. "I told Michael we were meeting Bryce here at midnight. Obviously he's found something better to do." Putting his hand on Katrina's tiny waist, he helped her into Bryce's car. "I just wish he'd had the courtesy to let one of us know so we wouldn't stick around waiting," Kenny complained, getting in after her.

"I hate to leave them stranded here," Leah said, hesitating.

"Come on, Leah. We've waited long enough," Katrina urged.

Leah stepped in and shut the door. As the car began to roll, she saw Kenny casually slip his arm around Katrina. Then, to Leah's surprise, Katrina leaned her head against his chest.

When they reached the girls' dorm, Bryce stopped only for a minute. Then he took off, leaving Kenny to walk Leah and Katrina to the door of their dorm.

"Well," Kenny said, rocking back and forth on his heels, "here we are."

Leah waited a second for him to leave for his dorm. Then she realized that both Kenny and Katrina were waiting for her to leave. Apparently they wanted to kiss each other good-night without Leah for an audience.

"Good night," she said softly, feeling a little foolish. Then she slipped through the glass door and hurried up the stairs to the third floor.

Leah got into her nightgown and was in bed by the time Katrina made it upstairs. Sweeping into the room, Katrina scooped up her pillow and began waltzing it around the room.

Finally Katrina collapsed on the window seat, still hugging the pillow tightly to her chest. "Oh, Leah, just look at that moon." Katrina sighed dreamily. "And to think I never noticed before."

"You never noticed the moon?" Leah teased her.

Katrina giggled. "No, I mean I never noticed Kenny. I never realized how wonderful he is, before tonight."

"Be careful, Katrina," Leah warned, only half joking. "You sound like you might be falling in love."

"I'm not *falling* in love," Katrina said with a sigh. "I *am* in love! I knew it the minute we kissed."

"I'm really happy for you, Katrina," Leah said as Katrina slipped into her own nightgown and got into her bed. Leah could remember how exciting it had been the first time she kissed Peter Forrest. But she couldn't help feeling a little sad about it, too. Kenny and Katrina had gotten closer tonight while she . . . she had no one.

Just then there was a muffled knock on the door. "Leah? Katrina? Are you awake?" Annie whispered.

Tossing off her covers, Katrina jumped up to get the door. "Where have you been?" she asked as the light from the hall flooded the darkened room.

Sitting up, Leah flicked on the light above her bed. "Yes, Annie. Where have you been?"

"You'll never guess," Annie said, waltzing into the room just as Katrina had done earlier. Then, not even waiting for them to try guessing, she said, "Michael took me to the Greenfield Inn for coffee and dessert. He said he's been wanting to go there ever since he saw a picture of the place in a brochure back in San Francisco."

"You might have told us where you were," Leah grumbled. "Bryce was pretty angry when you two didn't show up after the dance."

Annie looked surprised. "Oh, no! I guess my friend Julia didn't find Bryce, then. I asked her to tell him that Michael and I left early."

"It doesn't matter," Katrina assured her. "What matters is you and Michael. Did you have fun?"

"It was wonderful!" Annie exclaimed. "Michael is so easy to talk to. And boy, can he—"

"I'm exhausted, and we do have classes tomorrow as well as two performances," Leah interrupted. "I really need to get to sleep."

"I don't think I *can* sleep. Not yet anyway," Katrina declared.

"Me, neither," Annie agreed. Then her face brightened. "Why don't you come to my room, Katrina? Then we can talk, and Leah can sleep."

Katrina grinned. "Great idea. I'll grab my robe."

As soon as Katrina had slipped on her flannel bathrobe, Leah turned off the light and settled back in bed.

"Good night, Leah," Katrina said, pulling the door shut after her.

But once Leah was alone in the dark, she found she couldn't go to sleep. Leah could almost swear she could hear Annie and Katrina giggling, even though her door was closed. Leah tried to hug her pillow for comfort, but it didn't help much. Instead of having a great time with her friends in Vermont, Leah was lonely—very lonely. There was no other word for it.

Chapter 6

Saturday morning, when Michael entered the brightly lit studio on the top floor of the Greenfield College recital hall, Leah watched him with new interest. She decided she'd been taking him for granted, and not just as a partner. After all, he was a good-looking boy ... a good-looking man, she amended. He was eighteen now, two years older than she.

It was raining, and Leah had been performing a mixture of tendus, pliés, and relevés to the rhythm of the drops striking the skylight overhead, to keep her muscles warm for Madame's pas de deux workshop. Now she stopped.

Michael's brown eyes traveled around the studio, finally coming to rest on Leah. She smiled at him and waved, hoping he wouldn't notice the blush that sprang to her cheeks at the memory of the kiss she'd witnessed the night before. Michael returned Leah's wave, as if nothing unusual had happened, and began walking toward her.

"Hi," he said, stepping up to the barre, where Leah was stretching her foot.

"Hi," Leah responded. She certainly wasn't going to bring up the night before if he wasn't.

Placing his left hand on top of the barre, Michael began stretching his knees, rising upward to full demi-pointes. Then he slowly dropped his heels to the floor again as he continued down into a full plié. Leah watched this simple warmup with growing admiration. Then he stepped away from the barre and went into his preparation. Finally he did a series of turns à la seconde.

Leah clapped, shouting, "Great!"

Michael ended with a pirouette and glanced at Leah's reflection on the mirrored wall. "Are you making fun of me, Leah?" he asked suspiciously. "It wasn't that great," he said, tugging at the broad elastic folded up in the top of his black tights.

"No, you really did look great," Leah insisted. "You've gotten strong." Michael merely shrugged.

Madame walked into the studio, followed by the tall, thin accompanist, Roger Perry, who had been working with the class.

Madame sat down on the stool next to the piano and looked at the students gathering about her as Roger arranged his sheet music on the upright piano.

"Before we begin today, I want to remind you all of the story behind the pas de deux from *Coppélia* we are learning," Madame said. "The third act pas de deux is a prewedding dance. It is meant to be a dance of reconciliation and pledged happiness between Swanilda and Franz. This is a moving and emotional adagio, to be sure, but it does not have the tragic qualities of, say, *Giselle*.

"I hope you have all seen Joshua Showalter and Meredith Callan dance this pas de deux at some time, perhaps on "Dance in America." If you haven't, you might check the videos in the college library for a copy. I do not expect you to copy these principal dancers. I expect you to learn your own part of this pas de deux well enough to make it your own."

Then Madame clapped her hands, and the young dancers hurried to the barres that surrounded the mirrored room on three sides for more warm-ups, this time accompanied by Roger.

When Madame decided they were sufficiently warmed up, she had them break into pairs and begin marking the steps of the pas de deux. "One, two, three, four, five, six, lift!" Madame called out, keeping time with staccato claps of her hands.

After running through the dance several times, Madame singled out Michael and Leah. "You two will now dance full-out for the others," she told them.

After a quick trip to the rosin box Leah moved to the right and Michael to the center of the room. At Madame's prompting, Roger began playing Swanilda's entering music. But before Leah had finished counting out the beginning measures, the door to the studio began to open slowly, distracting her.

"Wait, Roger," Madame Preston commanded. Then, turning her full attention to the door, Madame said, "Come in. You may sit along this wall."

Several dancers Leah recognized as City Ballet apprentices and corps members entered the room. They were wearing an assortment of leotards, tights, leg warmers, and torn sweatshirts and had obviously just come from a workshop of their own. Annie, Leah noted, was among them.

Once the group was seated, Madame signaled

Roger to begin again. Leah tried to surrender herself to the music, but she felt stiff. She certainly didn't feel as if she and her Franz had reconciled. Michael was supposed to have his attention on Leah, but instead, he was grinning foolishly at Annie.

Leah's opening steps felt awkward, but she was determined to win back Michael's attention. She ran across the room toward Michael, who was to lift her high into the air above his head. But as Leah reached Michael, he didn't seem ready for his lift. She held back for a split second, afraid to trust him, forcing Michael to come forward slightly to get his hands around her for the lift. Leah felt her feet leave the ground. Then suddenly she fell to the floor.

"Leah! Are you okay?" Michael asked. He was hovering over her, holding out his hand.

Looking up, she cried, "You dropped me!" She felt a surge of anger. Michael had been watching Annie when he was supposed to be watching her! "It was all your fault!" she accused him.

"Are you all right, Leah?" Madame asked gently.

Leah thought for a moment. "I ... I think I'm okay," she answered shakily, her hands automatically going to her left foot, the one she had injured that spring. Her pride was hurt, but aside from the bruise she'd undoubtedly have on her tailbone, Leah seemed to be all right.

Annie came over and stood next to Michael. "Here, Leah, let me help you up," she offered.

"No, thank you. I'm *fine*," Leah insisted. She struggled to her feet, then added, "No thanks to Michael."

"Now wait a minute. This was as much your

fault as it was mine, Leah," he declared firmly. "You counted wrong. You weren't in the right place for the lift when the music called for it. I had to overcompensate, and I lost my balance."

"Now, now," Madame said, stepping between Michael and Leah. "Assigning blame will not undo anything. Thank goodness Leah isn't hurt. Now, return to your places, and Roger will begin again."

"I won't," Leah said. Then, seeing the beginnings of anger in Madame's eyes, Leah amended, "I mean, I don't think I can, Madame Preston."

"All right, then," Madame agreed reluctantly. "You and Michael may sit out."

"*I* don't need to sit out," Michael protested stubbornly.

"Could I try the pas de deux with Michael, Madame?" Annie asked.

For a minute or two Madame considered Annie's proposal. "Well," she finally said, "I suppose that would be interesting for all of us, my dear." Then she actually smiled at Annie. Leah felt as though someone had stuck a pin in her heart.

As Annie and Michael went hand in hand to join the others who were breaking into groups to dance full-out, Katrina approached Leah. "Are you sure you're okay, Leah?"

"Yes," Leah said, rubbing her arm. "I'm sure." Then she slowly walked to the piano, where she'd left her dance bag. Sinking onto the floor, Leah began unlacing her pointe shoes. Then she slipped her foot out from beneath the elastic. Finally she pulled out her pink-and-red I-love-San-Francisco sweatshirt and slipped it on. She hadn't worked up a sweat, but she still felt chilled.

Leah watched disinterestedly as a couple she

didn't really know danced full-out. They were adequate, she decided, arching her foot to keep it from cramping, but definitely uninspired.

Then it was Annie and Michael's turn. Leah was prepared to be critical of their dancing, but she found that impossible. Dancing to the Delibes score, they were as magical as they had been the night before in the park. Seeing them dance reminded Leah of the way she'd felt when she danced the pas de deux from *Romeo and Juliet* with James Cummings.

As soon as the dance was over, wild applause broke out. Even Leah had to admit the pair deserved it.

"You are right to clap," Madame told the class, smiling. "These two have shown a rare rapport with each other."

When the workshop was over, Leah dashed into the dressing room and grabbed her sandals. She planned to go straight back to the dorm and soak in a hot tub to ease her stiff, sore muscles before the two o'clock matinee that afternoon. With her purple carryall over her shoulder and her sandals in her hand, Leah hurried down the hall of the music building, nearly as anxious to avoid both Annie and Michael as she was to get into the only bathtub on the third floor of the dorm for a soothing soak.

"Leah, wait!" The sound of Katrina's voice made Leah stop. Leah turned around, expecting to see just Katrina hurrying after her. But Annie was with her.

"You're all right, aren't you?" Katrina sounded concerned.

Leah nodded. She was a little embarrassed by

her outburst during the workshop, especially since no one but the other SFBA students knew of the injury that had kept her from dancing for nearly two months. She was afraid she'd sounded temperamental and spoiled.

"Good," Annie said quickly. "Then you'll still be able to come with us to Miss Lobinskya's for tea!" Annie smiled at Leah as if nothing out of the ordinary had just happened in the pas de deux workshop.

"Oh?" Leah asked. "When were we invited?"

"Last night," Annie replied brightly. "Didn't I tell you? Well, anyway, while Michael and I were at the Greenfield Inn, we ran into Madame Preston and Miss Lobinskya. Miss Lobinskya invited us then. Actually she wanted Kenny and Michael to come, too, but they have another special men's workshop now." Annie shook her head sadly. "I wish we weren't all so busy."

Having tea with anyone, even Miss Lobinskya, was the last thing Leah wanted at the moment. She particularly didn't want to go with Annie, who was clearly doing her best to take away Leah's pas de deux partner. But Leah felt she had no choice.

"I'll go," Leah said halfheartedly. "But I need to shower first."

Katrina grinned. "Great! This is going to be fun!"

Chapter 7

By the time the girls arrived at Miss Lobinskya's cottage, the rain had started up again. Hopping out of the car Miss Lobinskya had sent for them, the three girls made a dash for the door. Miss Lobinskya opened it quickly.

"Well, it could be nicer now, couldn't it?" she asked cheerfully as the girls wiped their feet on the doormat. "Come on in, I have just the thing to cheer you up. Good strong tea and some scrumptious biscuits Madame brought me from a shop in San Francisco."

As Miss Lobinskya led the way into her cozy living room, Leah stole a quick glance at Annie. If only Annie weren't there, both the company and the setting would have been perfect, she thought to herself.

"I have everything ready in the kitchen," Miss Lobinskya said, motioning the girls to sit down.

"I'll help you," Katrina offered.

"I can help, too," Leah put in, not wanting to be left alone with Annie. Leah had a lot on her mind, but she didn't want to get into what had happened earlier in pas de deux class with Annie, not now. But before Leah could stand up, Miss Lobinskya waved her back down.

"No, two of us can handle things," she said. "I am not *so* old yet." She chuckled, her dark eyes sparkling in a way that reminded Leah of Mrs. Hanson, her housemother.

As soon as Leah and Annie were alone, Leah began squirming restlessly in the overstuffed chair. But it was soon apparent that Annie had no more interest in talking to Leah than Leah had in talking to her. Annie let out a few deep, dramatic sighs, but that was it.

Finally Leah looked over in Annie's direction. The older girl was sitting hunched over, her head resting in her hands, staring out the window. She looked terribly sad.

"Is something wrong?" Leah asked.

It seemed to take a great deal of effort on Annie's part to pull her eyes away from the rain running down the window. "Don't you see, Leah?" she said softly. "It's all so hopeless."

"What is? Tell me what you're talking about," Leah said.

"Dancing with Michael last night and again today was wonderful. I feel like we were made for each other. But what good is finding the perfect partner at a two-week festival? Soon we'll be three thousand miles apart again." A tear ran slowly down Annie's pale cheek.

It wasn't the first time Leah had seen Annie MacPhearson cry. In fact, tears had been Annie's favorite ploy back at Hannah Greene's. Whenever things weren't going her way in ballet class, Annie had cried.

Leah glared at Annie suspiciously. "If Michael's such a perfect partner for you, why don't you get him to try out for the New York City Ballet?" she asked, half joking.

But Annie either didn't hear the sarcasm in Leah's suggestion or else chose to ignore it. "Oh, Leah!" she exclaimed. "You're absolutely brilliant! That's what I should do. There are people at this festival who have the power to make a decision about Michael. It certainly can't hurt to suggest they watch him perform. Perhaps I can even arrange a special audition for him right now!" Annie stood up and surveyed the room eagerly. "I don't see the telephone," she said after a moment. "Did you see a telephone in here?"

"Why don't you ask Miss Lobinskya," Leah said, barely able to mask her anger.

Still undaunted, Annie practically skipped out of the room. Leah was only alone a few seconds before Katrina returned carrying a beautiful antique silver tea service. She set the tray on the large oak coffee table in front of the couch and sat down.

"Don't you think Annie's acting funny? Riding out here, she seemed really upset, and now she looks all excited. What's going on?" Katrina asked. "Have you two finally settled your differences?"

"Hardly. Annie's up to her old tricks, that's all," Leah replied.

"What do you mean, Leah? What tricks?" Katrina asked.

"Ever since we were little girls, she's always had to be first. She even left Hannah Greene's first," Leah grumbled.

Katrina shook her head. "Of course she did. Annie is older than you."

"But it's more than that, don't you see? Annie

went to New York when she was *fourteen.* I didn't leave San Lorenzo until I was *fifteen.*"

"Leah, you're being silly!"

"Am I? Well, now for some reason Annie's decided she wants Michael Litvak to be her partner for life. That's where she ran off to. She's calling the bigwigs at City Ballet to talk them into giving him an audition."

"Really? But that's wonderful! They look so good together. It would probably help both their careers if they were in the same company. I bet Michael will be thrilled when he finds out," Katrina said excitedly.

"Michael's *my* partner," Leah insisted. "He came to Summer Dance to partner me!"

Katrina shook her head. "You should hear how you sound, Leah."

"I suppose you think Annie has more of a right to dance with Michael than I do because of the *magic* that exists between them," Leah said.

"When we were talking on the plane trip out here, you didn't sound like you thought dancing with Michael was all that special," Katrina pointed out. "What's made you change your mind? Jealousy, or a genuine change of heart?"

"Whose friend are you anyway, Katrina?" Leah demanded.

"Yours *and* Annie's. I told you that last night," Katrina replied.

"Girls, girls!" Miss Lobinskya chided them as she swept into the room carrying a second tray, filled with tiny sandwiches and assorted English tea biscuits. "I could hear your voices all the way in the kitchen. I don't know what you were saying, but I could tell that it wasn't pleasant."

Katrina's face turned a brilliant red, and Leah felt herself flush as well. "We're sorry," they both muttered, nearly in unison.

"It's the rain that does it," Miss Lobinskya declared, gazing sadly out the cottage windows at the thick woods that bordered her tidy little yard and garden. She sat down on the couch next to Katrina and began to pour tea. She was just about to set the pot down when Annie returned.

Annie didn't offer an account of her phone call, but from the subdued look on her face, Leah suspected that it hadn't been all good. Leah was curious, but she wasn't about to ask and risk starting in on another argument about Michael in front of their dignified hostess.

After they had sampled the tea and biscuits, Annie said, "I couldn't help noticing your picture gallery when I went in the other room to make my call, Miss Lobinskya."

The Englishwoman smiled. "I've quite a collection of handsome partners, don't I, Annie?"

"Did you ever fall in love with any of them?" Leah suddenly blurted.

"Leah!" Katrina cried.

Reaching across the table to pat the back of Leah's hand reassuringly, Miss Lobinskya said, "It's quite all right, Katrina. It is a perfectly fair question for one dancer to ask another, particularly if one of the dancers is as young as Leah."

"Well, did you?" Annie pressed.

"Yes, I did. Every last one of them. At least everyone whose picture is hanging in the study," Miss Lobinskya confessed, her almond-shaped eyes taking on a faraway look.

"But was there one, you know, one special one?" Annie asked.

"Yes, there was," Miss Lobinskya answered. "But of course I didn't know it at the time. I'm afraid we never do—at least, most of us don't."

"Can you tell us who it was?" Leah pressed.

"The first, of course. There is never another quite like the first." Miss Lobinskya sighed. Then suddenly she clapped her hands together. "Enough of this. As I was saying earlier, it's the rain that's made us all so maudlin, but I have the perfect cure. We have a good hour before we must leave for the theater. How would you girls like to do a bit of rummaging while I tidy up the tea things?"

"We can't let you do all the cleaning up," Katrina declared. "We'll all help. It'll go faster that way."

Miss Lobinskya smoothed Katrina's bangs from her forehead. "I don't hurry anymore, my dear. So, you see, I'm perfectly content to putter in the kitchen for as long as it takes to get the job done. Come along, the three of you." She stood up and they followed her down the hall to a closed door.

"The attic," Miss Lobinskya announced as she produced a good-sized skeleton key from the pocket of her apron. Then she unlocked the door and led the way up the steep stairs.

The sound of rain pelting the roof was quite pronounced in the attic, making it seem warm and cozy. Along one wall hung several wardrobe bags, and a few wooden chests were arranged at one end of the room. In addition there were stacks and stacks of assorted hatboxes.

"These are some of my memorabilia," Miss Lobinskya told them, glancing around the room. "Digging around up here almost always cheers

me up, and I'm sure it will do the same for you."
She started backing slowly down the stairs. "I'll
call you when it's time to go. Enjoy!" Then she
left.

"Oh, look!" Katrina cried from the corner, where
she'd just unzipped one of the clothes bags. "Old
gowns!"

"Let's try them on," Annie suggested.

"Come on, Leah," Katrina said, pulling out a
beautiful black beaded dress with silver fringe.
"This looks just right for you!"

After hesitating a moment, Leah quickly slipped
out of her shorts and oversize T-shirt and into
the old dress. It fit perfectly. Pulling out the elastic
that was holding her hair back in a ponytail, Leah
let her long hair cascade about her shoulders.
Then she stepped over to the gilded mirror to
look at herself.

"Try this one, Katrina," Annie ordered, pulling
out an evening gown of pale blue taffeta. Katrina
slipped into the dress, then joined Leah at the
mirror.

"I feel like we've traveled back in time," Katrina
told Leah. She turned back to Annie. "Put something
on, Annie, and join us."

"I'm still looking, but I don't think anything
here will fit me. I'm taller than you two, and
nothing here is cut right for me." Then, pulling a
bright green feather boa from the bag, Annie threw
it around her shoulders like a shawl.

"That color really makes your hair look red,
Annie. I love it!" Katrina cried.

Annie looked thoughtfully at Katrina. "You could
use some color yourself, Katrina. For starters, you
should be doing something to make the most of

those big brown eyes of yours. Then you might think about perking up your pale complexion, you know, with a little base and some blush."

Katrina frowned. "I wear makeup on stage, but I don't like it. I feel like I'm wearing a mask."

"You are when you're on stage. But I'm not talking about heavy, theatrical makeup—just a little everyday lift. Leah, you know what I mean, don't you?" Annie asked.

Leah shrugged. She'd been blessed with a lot of natural coloring and usually only wore a little blush and a hint of violet eye shadow.

She didn't like to admit that Annie was right, but Katrina did look washed out, even though it was the middle of summer. "You could try wearing a little blush," she told Katrina gently.

Annie pulled off the feather boa and draped it over Katrina's shoulders. "I'm going to run downstairs and get my makeup case. I think I have just the stuff to awaken your sleeping beauty, Katrina," she added as she started down the stairs.

Leah walked back across the attic, slipped out of the beaded dress and back into her own clothes. Before she was finished changing, Annie was back, makeup case in hand.

"Sit here, Katrina," Annie commanded, pulling a stool over to the mirror. "And take a good look at yourself. Otherwise, by the time I'm finished, you'll have forgotten what you looked like."

Katrina giggled. "Just don't make me look unreal, you know, like a doll."

"Looking like a doll is all right," Annie assured her, "if it's a *living* doll." Both girls giggled. Then Annie got to work.

Leah wandered away from Katrina's make-over.

She looked around the attic further and discovered a satin-lined box of costume jewelry. She tried on a pair of earrings and a delicate tiara. But without a friend to giggle with, it wasn't much fun.

With the excited banter between Katrina and Annie in the background, Leah moved on to a small pile of shoe boxes. Each box was tied up with a pink satin ribbon. Leah sat down on the floor and put the top box on her lap. Carefully she removed the ribbon and took the lid off the box. Inside were several letters that had yellowed with age. Sensing that the content of the letters was private, Leah was about to replace the lid when Annie ran over to her.

"Old letters!" she cried. "I'll bet they're love letters!" Leah tried to put the box back in the stack, but Annie snatched it from her.

"Put it away," Leah demanded. "Those letters are private. Reading them would be wrong."

For a second Annie gave Leah a withering look. Then she said, "Miss Lobinskya herself gave us permission to rummage around up here. If she hadn't wanted us to read these, she would have said so."

"Miss Lobinskya probably just assumed that we would have the common decency not to snoop into her private correspondence," Leah argued.

"I think Annie is right," Katrina said, coming over to stand beside Annie. "Miss Lobinskya told us we could look at anything up here that interested us."

Meanwhile Annie had pulled the top letter out of its tattered envelope. "I can't believe this," she moaned, sinking to the floor as she kept reading. "This letter is so incredibly sad!" She set the letter down on the floor next to her and pulled out the next one. Annie sniffled.

"What's wrong, Annie?" Katrina asked. She sat down next to Annie and slipped a comforting arm around her shoulders.

"The life of a ballerina is so sad," Annie muttered, shaking her head.

"What are you talking about?" Leah asked.

"She knew all those wonderful danseurs in the photographs downstairs, all her old partners. Yet, in her old age, she's all alone. Don't you see? No matter how well she may have danced with any one of them, eventually she left them."

"But she had choices," Leah protested. "And anyway, she seems happy to me."

"What's really troubling you, Annie?" Katrina prompted gently. "Is it Michael?"

Annie nodded. "I think I'm in love with Michael. And a week from now we'll be saying good-bye to each other . . . maybe forever!"

"In love!" Leah exclaimed. "But that's ridiculous. You just met Michael a few days ago. How can you possibly know that you love him?"

"Some things don't take *time* to know," Annie said forlornly. "Love is one of those things."

Carefully Annie slipped the two letters back in their envelopes and put them back in the shoe box. She then handed the box to Leah. "I called about the audition, as you suggested, Leah, but the chances of something happening here in the next week are slim. Then Michael and I will be on opposite sides of the country again."

"It's easy to think you're in love when you dance well with someone," Leah said, thinking of the way she'd felt about both Andrei Levintoff and James Cummings while she'd been working with them. "But I'm afraid dancing and romance don't mix well."

Annie frowned. "What do you mean?"

"Remember when Alex thought she was in love, Katrina?" Leah asked, finding it easier at the moment to talk about their Russian friend than about herself. "She gave up her career in ballet because of Ben Lydgate, because she thought they were in love. Now they don't even see each other anymore."

"But Ben Lydgate isn't a dancer," Katrina pointed out logically. "Things would be different for Annie and Michael."

Annie sighed. "If we could only be together all the time!"

Leah gave up. If Annie didn't want her advice, she wasn't going to force it on her.

"Girls, it's time to leave for the matinee!" Miss Lobinskya called up to them.

"Come on," Katrina said, smiling at Annie and Leah. "Let's go. Everything will work out, Annie."

"One way or the other," Leah couldn't help adding.

Chapter 8

There wasn't a cloud in the dazzlingly blue Vermont sky the next day as Leah left the campus to walk to the festival picnic in Rose Park. Annie and Katrina had offered to wait for her, but she'd insisted she'd find them later. She knew she needed some time alone to collect her thoughts.

Leah was anxious to find Michael at the picnic. She wanted to have a word with him alone. She'd been thinking about their pas de deux class the Saturday morning that she'd fallen, and she decided she owed him an apology. She hoped he'd understand how frightened she had been when she fell, because of the serious injury she'd suffered not too long ago.

Now that the sun was out again, Leah discovered she felt much better about everything. Miss Lobinskya had been right, she decided, taking a playful little leap over the remains of a puddle. Rainy days could bring out the worst in a person. Today Leah was even sorry she hadn't been more understanding up in Miss Lobinskya's attic when Annie said she was upset about leaving Michael.

When Leah finally reached the park, it was already crowded. She recognized several dancers from the classes and workshops she'd been taking, and waved to them. Then she saw Miss Moraldi and Bryce Coleman near the pavilion, talking to Miss Lobinskya. She was about to go over to talk with them when she heard someone calling her name.

Leah turned and saw Katrina waving at her. "Over here!" Katrina said. She was standing under a tree in the shade with Kenny.

"Hi," Leah said, joining them. "Have you guys seen Michael?"

Kenny motioned toward the lake. "Michael took Annie down there. The rowboat rental is open today, and Annie wanted a ride." He slipped a proprietary arm around Katrina's shoulders. "We're headed that way ourselves. Want to go out in a boat with us, Leah?" he offered.

Leah shook her head, trying not to let Kenny and Katrina see how disappointed she was that Michael was already with Annie. She didn't want to talk to him in front of Annie, and now she'd have to wait. "Three's a crowd, especially in a little boat on a small lake," she told them. "I think I'll wander over there and watch the game."

Katrina shrugged. "We'll see you later, then. Come on, Kenny."

Kenny looked back over his shoulder at Leah and winked as Katrina led him toward the lake. Leah sighed. She hadn't minded walking to the park alone, but now she felt lonely again. It seemed as if everyone was paired up this summer ... everyone except her.

"Here's Leah now!" Madame Preston's voice boomed from right behind Leah, causing her to jump. Madame chuckled. "Forgive me for startling you, Leah. I simply wanted to introduce you to the Talbots. This is Leah Stephenson. Leah was our Golden Gate recipient last year."

The words *last year* startled Leah even more than Madame's voice had seconds earlier. Those two little words made Leah feel like a has-been. As she shook hands with the distinguished-looking older couple, Leah realized she needed a new accomplishment to make her interesting again.

As if to confirm Leah's suspicion that she was uninteresting, Mrs. Talbot looked right over Leah's head and said, "Isn't that Ashley Phillips over there? Do you think you might introduce us to *her*?"

"Of course. It would be my pleasure," Madame assured her pleasantly. Then turning to Leah, Madame said, "Would you like to come with us, Leah? I know Ashley would enjoy seeing you again."

"No, thank you, Madame," Leah replied politely. "I was on my way to play croquet." Then she remembered to add, "It was a pleasure to meet you, Mr. and Mrs. Talbot."

But the Talbots were already walking toward Ashley Phillips and didn't seem to hear her. Madame smiled at Leah as if to say, "They're patrons. They can afford to be rude, but we cannot." Then she followed the Talbots through the crowd.

Leah turned and started weaving her way through the crowd, when she noticed that several people were holding plates of food. Since she hadn't had much to eat except a light supper the night before, Leah decided to head to the food table.

Leah joined the line, behind Bryce Coleman.

"Hi, Leah," Bryce greeted her cheerfully. "Recovered from our night of dancing under the stars?" he asked, giving her a playful wink.

Leah noticed a stuffy-looking couple in line in front of Bryce start to look from Leah to Bryce and back again. Leah could easily imagine the kind of gossip that would get passed around because of Bryce's innocent teasing.

"How is Christina anyway?" Leah asked, hoping to put a stop to any rumors by mentioning the ballerina she'd heard he was dating.

Bryce scowled and shook his head. "As temperamental as ever, I'm afraid," he said, making Leah laugh. When she laughed, Bryce did, too.

The line crept slowly forward. Eventually Leah was able to take a plate. Then she paused to survey the sumptuous offering that included everything from Russian caviar and tiny pastry puffs loaded with lobster salad to bowls of fresh strawberries and other seasonal fruit. It wasn't long before Leah had filled her plate and was searching for a spot to sit down and enjoy the feast.

Leah was spreading caviar on a cracker when she heard the park's public address system crackle to life.

Suddenly Miss Lobinskya's delightful voice, with its clipped British accent, could be heard above all the other conversations. "I have an important and exciting announcement to make," she said. "The other festival directors and I have decided to hold a special student performance next Sunday afternoon at two o'clock. We had originally thought we wouldn't be able to offer this closing-day gala until next year. But due to the magnificent promise shown by our youngest participants, we've moved this special feature of the Summer Dance festival up a year." Miss Lobinskya paused while the crowd broke into an enthusiastic round of applause.

"Participation in this special performance," Miss Lobinskya continued, "is open to all our Summer Dance participants, both students and professionals, who are under the age of twenty-one and are not yet soloists or principals with companies. Auditions will be held Thursday afternoon on the stage of the Performing Arts Center. I want to encourage every young person to try out. I also want to encourage all you marvelous patrons, dance critics, artistic directors, and so forth to be sure to be in attendance next Sunday. I'm sure you will welcome this rare opportunity to preview tomorrow's stars." There was more applause; then Miss Lobinskya added, "Everyone who can manage to stay after the two o'clock performance is also invited to a closing gathering that will be held in the main house of the Ado estate. Now, back to your picnicking, everyone. Please don't forget to take a walk through the rose gardens at the southeastern corner of the park." As Miss Lobinskya stepped down from the microphone, the crowd erupted in still more thunderous applause.

Only Leah didn't seem thrilled by the announcement of the upcoming auditions and performance. Before Saturday's disaster in the pas de deux workshop, Leah would immediately have thought of auditioning the third-act adagio from *Coppélia* with Michael. They had been the best couple in the workshop until Annie had interfered.

Leah dropped her half-eaten cracker on her

plate. She'd lost her appetite. With the auditions open to professional dancers, Leah didn't see how she stood a chance of getting to perform anyway. Even if she and Michael could somehow manage to dance as well together as they had been dancing back at SFBA, they weren't professional quality yet.

"Oh, Leah, isn't it wonderful?" Katrina asked, rushing over to Leah just as she was about to throw the rest of her picnic lunch into the trash bin.

"I guess so," Leah said indifferently. It was easy for Kenny and Kartrina to be excited, she told herself. They actually stood a chance of getting to perform. But Leah was afraid she and Michael were hopeless.

"I've never seen as many important people gathered in one place before," Kenny said excitedly. "The Sunday performance could be the sort of opportunity we're all looking for."

"You're absolutely right, Kenny. I think I'm dreaming!" Annie said from behind Leah. Spinning around, Leah glared at Annie. "I had heard some rumors about this," Annie went on, undaunted, "but I thought that if it was really going to happen, Madame Preston would have told you guys about it sooner. Do you realize we only have four days until auditions?"

"But we've been working all week," Michael pointed out, sounding both solid and sensible. Leah smiled at him. She couldn't help noticing how great he looked in his faded jeans and loose-fitting striped T-shirt.

"That's right," Leah agreed, suddenly hopeful. They *had* been working all week. They would audition the pas de deux from *Coppélia* together after all! Leah looked at Michael fondly.

Annie shook her head and sighed dramatically. "I suppose you're right, Michael. We'll have to do something we've been working on. I suppose that means I'll have to audition the solo from *Giselle*." She laid her hand lightly on Michael's arm. "If only we had time to work on the second act pas de deux from *Giselle* together! We'd really impress the bigwigs from City Ballet with that. I'm sure the right people will be at the performance next Sunday, too."

Leah scowled. Michael didn't know *Giselle* any more than she did. They wouldn't be working on that ballet at SFBA until the fall. Leah knew that Michael had been as excited about working on *Giselle* with Madame Preston as she had.

"But Michael is *my* partner!" Leah sputtered.

Michael looked shocked by her outburst. "I'm getting a little tired of your attitude, Leah. You act like you own me or something!"

Then, not waiting for her to respond, Michael took Annie by the hand and led her away.

"I just wish you'd stop all this, Leah," Katrina said. "Why can't you just let Michael and Annie be happy? You aren't in love with Michael. You told me so yourself on the plane ride out here. Why can't you accept that Annie loves Michael?"

"That's not the point," Leah protested softly. "Madame brought Michael here as *my* partner. Annie isn't even a student at SFBA."

"I think you're wrong, Leah," Kenny said carefully. "Madame didn't bring Michael here just because of you. She brought him because he's a good dancer. You just happen to have been paired in pas de deux class back at SFBA and here as well. But pas de deux is only one of the classes Michael's taking here. It's not his life."

Katrina nodded. "Kenny's right, Leah. You're still not giving Michael as much credit as he deserves. I'm not surprised he's angry with you."

Leah started to protest again, but neither Katrina nor Kenny was willing to listen to her. "We're going to get something to eat," Kenny said, cutting her off midsentence. "Want to come with us?"

"Leah already ate," Katrina pointed out coldly before Leah could respond to Kenny's invitation.

"Oh, well. We'll see you later, then, Leah." Kenny smiled; then he and Katrina walked away.

Alone again, Leah felt more confused than ever. She knew she didn't own Michael, and she couldn't understand why he'd even suggested that she thought she did. It was Annie who wanted to own Michael. But so far, Leah hadn't been able to point that out to anyone else, not even Katrina.

Annie might be pretending she loved Michael. But Leah knew the truth. Annie was just using Michael to further her own career. She didn't really care about him.

Leah was so upset that she decided to return to her room on the Greenfield campus, where she could be alone. As she walked through the crowd still milling about Rose Park, Leah thought about her cozy third-floor room at Mrs. Hanson's boardinghouse. She missed her little cat, Misha. In fact, she missed everything about San Francisco. One more week, she told herself, one more long week! Then she could go back to California where she belonged!

Chapter 9

Monday afternoon Leah leaned against the barre to catch her breath while Michael stalked over to the piano to rewind their rehearsal tape. She watched Michael in the wall mirror as he took the tape out of the machine and flipped it over.

"What are you doing?" Leah demanded. So far, their work had been just barely satisfactory. Leah had the feeling that Michael was holding something back. Now he seemed to be wasting their precious rehearsal time playing with the tape. The auditions were Thursday; they only had two sessions after this one to make sure they got it right.

"I was just trying to see what was on the other side of this tape. Nothing, I guess," Michael said with a shrug. Then he slipped the tape back in the recorder and pushed the rewind button.

As she listened to the mechanical whir of the tape machine, Leah lifted her leg, hooking her heel on the barre. Then she slowly lowered her head to her ankle. Meanwhile Michael pulled off his leg warmers and his old brown sleeveless sweatshirt. Leah hoped that meant he was finally ready to get down to business. After all, this adagio was supposed to symbolize the reconciliation between two lovers. But so far, Leah felt they'd been dancing as if the ballet were about two strangers meeting on a bus—and not too happily at that.

"Ready?" Michael asked, his finger poised above the tape player.

Leah nodded as she lowered her leg from the barre. Michael pressed the play button, and immediately the small studio was filled with the Delibes score for *Coppélia*. Michael bowed and held out his hand to Leah.

Everything seemed to be going well through the first few lifts. But then, as Michael caught Leah, the blank look Leah saw in his eyes filled her with rage. He was asleep; he wasn't even trying to dance well. Pulling away from him, Leah stomped across the room and snapped off the tape.

"What's wrong?" Michael demanded.

"You, that's what. You're acting like you've got the flu," Leah said accusingly.

"Frankly, I'm just not inspired," Michael retorted with anger equal in intensity to Leah's.

Leah felt stung. How dare he say that to her? Turning away from him, she flung open the studio door. Immediately she saw Annie sitting in a folding chair right next to the entrance!

"Hi, Leah," Annie said cheerfully. Her tone made Leah feel even madder than she already was.

Putting her hands on her hips, Leah glared at Annie. "What are you doing here?" she asked, tapping her pointed shoe impatiently on the floor.

"I have a surprise for Michael," Annie replied. Then she looked down at her watch. "You aren't finished rehearsing, are you? I thought you had this room until five o'clock."

"Annie!" Michael cried, finally coming out into the hall. "I'm so glad to see you!" Bending down, he gave Annie a quick kiss on the cheek. Michael certainly seemed inspired about that, Leah noted bitterly. "What are you doing here?"

"That's what I want to know," Leah exclaimed.

"I've got exciting news," Annie said. Then she looked at Leah. "But it can wait if you're not through."

"We're supposed to rehearse another half hour," Michael said. He gave Leah a dirty look. "But Leah—"

"Was just catching her breath," Leah said with new determination. She certainly wasn't going to give up their valuable rehearsal time so that Michael and Annie could flirt with each other. "I'm ready now, though. Let's get back to work, Michael."

"I want to hear Annie's news. You go back in," he virtually ordered Leah. "I'll be back in a minute."

Indignant at the way Michael was treating her but feeling she had no choice if she wanted to continue to rehearse, Leah went back in the room, closing the door behind her. But Michael didn't come back in a minute.

After five minutes had passed, Leah pulled on her lavender sweatshirt to keep her muscles from tightening up. She refused to give either Annie or Michael the satisfaction of forcing her to go back out in the hall to fetch Michael.

Finally, a full ten minutes later, Michael came sauntering back in, looking starry-eyed. Leah was furious. She wanted to tell Michael off, but that would only take more of their time.

Walking across the wooden floor, Leah punched the recorder's rewind button. Then she took a couple of more steps to the rosin box and began angrily grinding first one toe shoe and then the other in the little sticky chunks.

Finally she turned back to Michael. "We've only fifteen minutes left," she said through clenched teeth. "Let's make the most of it."

"Madame Preston has agreed to let Annie teach me the pas de deux from *Giselle.* I'm going to dance with Annie, too," he told her.

Now Leah knew where the stars in Michael's eyes had come from. He was finally getting the chance to partner Annie!

"That's great, but now we're going on *Coppélia,*" Leah reminded him. "Let's keep our minds on that. Okay?"

"Okay. But I want to thank you first, Leah," Michael said, giving her a warm smile.

"Thank me? For what?" Leah was totally bewildered.

"Annie said you were the one who suggested I try out for City Ballet! When she told Madame that, Madame agreed to let us audition for the gala together."

"*Annie* told Madame that!" Leah cried.

"It was your idea, wasn't it?" Michael asked. He looked confused.

"Yes, but . . ." Leah began, but didn't finish. She realized it was futile to try to explain how she had said it but hadn't really meant it.

"Well, thank you." Michael smiled, making Leah hope that Annie's news might actually backfire on her. Michael seemed so happy, Leah thought he might dance better with her.

Unfortunately their dancing got worse instead of better, though. Each time Michael lifted Leah, she was certain he was going to drop her. When she pirouetted in his arms, it felt as though he was holding her too tightly, stopping her spin instead of supporting her.

By the time their rehearsal was over, Leah knew she was just as happy to have Michael run out to Annie's waiting arms as he was to go.

On her way back to her room after rehearsal, Leah stopped off at the mail room. Finding a letter waiting there for her was definitely the high point of Leah's day, particularly since it was from Kay.

After ripping the envelope as she walked toward her room, Leah pulled the letter out. Then she smiled. Kay's scratchy handwriting was as energetic as her dancing. Pausing to lean against the wall of the nearest building, Leah read:

Dear Leah,

I'm so glad you wrote to me right away. I've been meaning to write back, but I've been so busy that I've been falling asleep the minute I sit down.

I had dinner with Alex and her parents my first night in New York. They said they're going to try to get up to Greenfield for a weekend while you're there. Isn't that exciting? I told them you'd love it if they did. Alex wants to surprise you, so don't tell them I told you they were coming.

Anyway, Alex has seen James Cummings a

couple of times. Of course he asked about you. When she told him about Summer Dance, he was upset because his schedule with the Joffrey is so heavy right now that he can't break away to come up, not even for a day. Well, I suppose you're being swarmed by handsome partners up there, as usual, and would probably find a visit from James awkward anyway.

Alex says Pam has been writing to James! Can you believe that? That girl has a lot of nerve. Remember the time in pas de deux class when she gored him with her long fingernails and he dropped her? Anyway, in Pam's last letter she said she's the real star of that regional ballet company she's dancing with in Atlanta but was cheated out of the best role in whatever it is they're putting on now because of *unfair competition*. Doesn't that sound just like Pam? Nothing's ever *her* fault, is it?

I've gotten postcards from both Linda and Sophie. The dance camp with Diana Chang is really fun, according to them both. I guess the part of California they're in isn't at all like San Francisco ... it's sunny all the time! But you would know more about that than me, being a California girl.

In fact, it sounds like everyone is having more fun than I am! You and Katrina up there in the resort capital of the Northeast, and Linda, Sophie, and Suzanne living it up in Southern California at camp.

But don't get me wrong. Dana Daniels is totally awesome, and everything she has to say is inspiring. It's just that she has me taking so many classes, everything from t'ai chi to ethnic and modern dance. Then, of course, I have to take a ballet class every day. I think I'm simply too tired to enjoy this time with Dana as much as I might if it were spread out over a year instead of a few weeks.

Well, say hi to Katrina and Kenny, and give Michael a big hug for me. I'm sure, after your extra pas de deux work with Madame, you four are going to put the rest of us to shame when we start working on *Giselle* this fall. I miss you!

Love,
Kay

When Leah looked up from Kay's letter at the thick Vermont woods that surrounded the Greenfield College campus, she wished Kay were there that very moment so she could unburden her heart. How wrong she had been to think that two weeks at Summer Dance would be a vacation from the competition that clouded the otherwise perfect world of SFBA! All the things Leah had thought she was escaping actually seemed more intense here.

Leah thought about writing to Kay, but it seemed as if too much had happened since the first time she'd written for her to get it all down on paper. Sometime during the week, Leah vowed, she'd pick up a postcard in town and mail it off to Kay, just to let her know she'd gotten her letter and appreciated hearing from her.

Leah stuck the letter in the outside pocket of

her dance bag and started walking toward the dorm again. When she got up to the room, she found Katrina there, just getting ready to go out.

"I got a letter from Kay," Leah told her, pulling out the letter and holding it toward Katrina. "Want to read it?"

Katrina smiled. "Sure," she said. She took the letter over to her bed and sat down.

"Annie was telling me some more about New York this morning. It really sounds great," Katrina said as she refolded the letter and handed it back to Leah. "She says there's something happening every night of the week."

Leah felt like screaming. Couldn't they even share a letter from Kay without having it somehow tie in with Annie? Leah wanted to ask. But she knew if she said anything against Annie, whom Katrina had grown to admire so much, she would only be making herself look bad again.

"I miss Kay and Linda and everybody from the Academy, don't you, Leah?" Katrina asked as Leah carried the letter to her dresser and stuck it in the top drawer. "In some ways it feels like we've been here months instead of just one week."

Leah slid the drawer shut, then turned to face Katrina again. "It feels like that to me, too. In fact, I can hardly wait to get out of here. I think I'd leave tomorrow if I could."

"But what about all the great workshops? And aren't you excited about the performance next Sunday?" Katrina asked. "I think my parents are going to come down Saturday and spend the night. That way they can see me perform in the corps Saturday night and, I hope, in a pas de deux with Kenny Sunday. I think we actually have a chance, especially since we're auditioning with the second act pas de deux from *Swan Lake* that we both know so well already."

"I think you have more than just a chance," Leah told her honestly.

Katrina's pale cheeks colored with pleasure. "Thanks. But what about you and Michael, Leah? I'm sure if Kenny and I are chosen, you will be, too."

Leah shrugged. "Not necessarily. We really aren't dancing well together at all. I guess I feel that dancing with someone should be a shared experience, you know, like you say you're feeling with Kenny. But with Michael and me right now it's more of a fight than a dance."

"It's just the pressure. Maybe you should take some time off, Leah, to do something entirely different from ballet and relax. A bunch of us are going to this little café in town tonight where they have live music. They're supposed to have great desserts and fabulous iced cappuccino. Want to come?" Katrina asked.

"I suppose Annie and Michael are going," Leah ventured, trying to sound casual.

Katrina nodded. "But I'm sure Kenny can find a date for you, too, if you want to come. It'll be fun."

Leah knew Katrina meant well, but that didn't make her feel better. "There's nothing wrong with my dancing, Katrina, and I don't need Kenny's help finding a date, either," she told her friend.

"Okay, okay," Katrina said, backing toward the door. "Suit yourself." Then, pausing with her hand on the doorknob, Katrina added, "Oh, by the way, my parents said they'd pick us up late tomorrow afternoon. We'll have supper on the road so we can get to our farm while it's still early. Dad's bringing us back Wednesday in plenty of time for rehearsals and that compulsory seminar we all have to attend. You still want to see our farm, don't you, Leah?"

Leah felt stung that Katrina would even question her desire to visit the Grays' farm. "Of course, I do!" she insisted.

Katrina smiled. "Good. Because I want you to come. Well, see you later."

"Bye!" Leah called after her. When Katrina was gone, Leah looked around at the bare walls of their room. They never had gotten the posters they'd been planning to get. They probably never would now.

Leah got her last letter from Chrissy out of her dresser drawer. But even rereading a letter from her oldest and dearest friend didn't cheer her up.

Chapter 10

"*Doesn't this sun feel great?*" Katrina asked she rolled over onto her stomach on the sheet the girls had spread over the grass on the side of their dorm.

"You were right, Katrina," Leah told her. "Lying in the sun was a great idea." She splashed some suntan lotion on her bare legs and began rubbing it in. Then she lay back again, fanning her hair out around her head so the sun could shine on her face. She didn't add that Katrina had also been right about her needing to relax. She'd gone to bed early Monday night and was certain that the extra sleep had also helped calm her down.

"We might go swimming at the pond on our neighbors' farm tomorrow before we come back," Katrina said. "And I don't want Kenny to think I'm too pale when he sees me in my swimming suit."

Glancing over at Katrina, Leah noticed that she was already a little pink. Leah picked up the lotion and squirted some on Katrina's back.

"Hey!" Katrina cried, squirming slightly. "What are you doing?"

Leah laughed. "Putting some lotion on your back, silly. You don't want Kenny to think you're too sunburned, either."

Katrina giggled. "Thanks."

Leah lay down on the sheet. She felt lucky. Even though she had blond hair and blue eyes, Leah never sunburned. It was so nice to be outside in the fresh Vermont air.... Leah was half asleep when she suddenly felt a chill.

"Hi there! Sunbathing?" Opening her eyes, Leah saw Annie standing over her, creating a shadow. She sat up and slipped her hot-pink surfer shirt on over her turquoise-and-pink bikini.

"Hi, Annie," Katrina said brightly.

"I've been looking for you guys," Annie said. "I just realized it's Tuesday already, and I don't have anything to wear to the party after the gala Sunday. I wondered if you want to go shopping with me." Then she looked over at Leah. "But if you're busy ..." she added hesitantly.

"We were just relaxing for a little bit," Katrina said. "But I've had enough sun. If you can wait a minute, I'll go up to the room and slip on some clothes. Want to come, Leah?"

Leah shook her head. "I'm not really up for shopping right now. I think I'll stick with the sun."

"Okay. I'll be right back!" With that Katrina gathered up her things and dashed toward the nearest door of the dorm.

As soon as Katrina was gone, Annie sat down on the sheet with Leah. "Why are you sunbathing over here, Leah? There are a ton of people out on the green in the center of the campus. Wouldn't it be more fun over there?"

"Katrina said she felt more comfortable over here. She's kind of sensitive about her pale skin," Leah explained.

"Oh," Annie said. Then, after a moment she said, "So, are you excited?"

"About the auditions?" Leah asked carefully. Undoubtedly Michael had told Annie how terribly the two of them were dancing together these days, but she didn't think she wanted to discuss that with Annie.

Annie shook her head. "I'm not talking about the auditions. I'm talking about the trip to Katrina's farm this afternoon."

Leah felt her jaw drop as she realized what Annie was saying. "You mean, you're coming, too?" But before Annie could confirm Leah's fear, Katrina came back.

"I'm ready," Katrina announced.

"You look great, Katrina!" Annie cried, leaping to her feet. "Let's go."

"Are you sure you don't want to come?" Katrina asked Leah.

Leah nodded. "I'm sure."

"Okay. See you later," Katrina said.

As she watched the girls walk off in the direction of town, Leah felt terrible. It seemed that whenever she and Katrina were having fun together, Annie showed up and took Katrina away. They'd hardly spent any time together on this trip. And now Katrina had invited Annie to go with Kenny, Michael, and her to the Grays' farm for the night. Leah had hoped to have some time with Michael without Annie around. If they didn't get some things straightened out between them, and soon, Leah was afraid the auditions were going to be a disaster.

While Leah packed her dance bag for her Tuesday afternoon rehearsal with Michael, she reviewed her options. Maybe it would be better for her if she didn't dance with Michael after all. Certainly those making decisions at the auditions would see that Leah and Michael were out of sync with each other and wouldn't let them perform on Sunday anyway.

Leah slipped her denim miniskirt on over her dance clothes and slung her bag over her shoulder. If she didn't go to Katrina's farm that night, she just might be able to work on a solo for the audition.

Leah could probably do the Bluebird variation from *The Sleeping Beauty* she'd danced for her entrance audition to SFBA. She had spent so much time on that once, that pulling it back together would be relatively easy, she told herself, and it was a real showpiece for her form as well. Maybe Leah could even convince Bryce Coleman to give her a hand. After all, he'd been pretty friendly to Leah and seemed to like her dancing during the couple of classes she'd had with him so far.

Leah crossed the campus green so deep in thought that she barely noticed all the students around her having fun. A large group was tossing a Frisbee back and forth. Another group was gathered around a guitar player who was singing folk songs. Still others were stretched out on the lawn reading or merely soaking up the warm July sun.

But Leah was too determined even to consider doing any of those things herself. More than anything she wanted to be on the stage of the Greenfield Performing Arts Center on Sunday afternoon. Leah felt she needed to make the most of this opportunity to expand her horizons beyond the confines of the San Francisco Ballet Academy. And she was now ready to work harder than she'd ever worked before to realize her ambition.

By the time she reached the stairs to the music building, she was filled with new resolve. It was all beginning to make sense. Having Katrina invite Annie to her parents' house was only making it easier for Leah to do the right thing.

After stopping in the girls' dressing room long enough to slip out of her skirt and put her hair up in a neat chignon, Leah made her way to the practice room where she was scheduled to rehearse with Michael at four o'clock. As Leah neared the practice room, she heard the strains of the Delibes score through the slightly ajar practice room door. Taking her last few steps as quietly as she could, Leah peered in. There was Michael, alone in the room, walking through their pas de deux, a determined look on his angular features.

So, Michael was taking their audition piece seriously after all. Leah felt a curious mixture of embarrassment, anger, and frustration at the revelation. Now, if Leah told Michael she'd decided to dance a solo instead of a pas de deux with him, it would look as though she were acting out of spite over Michael's plans to partner Annie, too. And if she weren't going to change her audition piece from a pas de deux to a solo, telling Katrina that she wasn't going to the farm with the rest of them would also look as though her decision was based on jealousy of Annie. Leah was simply going to have to make the best of things.

She took a deep breath to calm herself. Then, with all the stage presence she'd learned during the past year at SFBA, she pushed the door open and walked into the room. "Hi," she said brightly.

"Hi." Michael crossed the room and clicked off the tape. "I think I've figured out a few things that will smooth out the rough edges. Shall I show you?"

Leah smiled. Maybe she'd been wrong to be so upset. Maybe everything was going to work out fine after all.

After an extremely successful rehearsal with Michael, Leah packed her carryall for the trip to the Grays' house. It seemed strange to be carrying a toothbrush, a nightgown, a change of clothes, and a swimming suit in her dance bag instead of her soft leather slippers, toe shoes, and other dance paraphernalia.

When they originally discussed going to Katrina's house, missing one morning class hadn't seemed like such a big deal. But now that the competition was proving to be just as stiff in Greenfield, Vermont, as it was in San Francisco, missing morning class and a workshop of character dancing seemed a bit risky to Leah. But she felt she had to go, if only to prove once and for all that Annie couldn't get the better of her.

"All set!" Leah told Katrina as she zipped her carryall closed.

"I am, too. Let's go, then. Annie went to get Michael and Kenny. Maybe they're even out front already."

Leah slung her bag over her shoulder. She reminded herself that she was going to have to get along with everyone on this trip. If there was any trouble of any kind, Leah feared she would be held accountable for it, whether it was her fault or not.

"I'm so glad you asked me along, Katrina," Annie said when Katrina and Leah joined Annie and the boys down at the parking lot. "I think a little break in the routine will help us all dance better."

"There's Dad now!" Katrina started waving madly at a beat-up–looking brown station wagon that was approaching the dorm.

The car came to a stop in front of the young dancers, and a tall, slender man stepped out. "Hi, Kat," he managed to say before Katrina leapt into his arms and gave him a fierce hug.

"Daddy!" she cried. "It's so good to see you! This is my dad," Katrina said to Leah and the others after her father had set her down. "And this is my little brother, Andrew." She put her arm around the shaggy-haired little boy who bore a strong resemblance to both Katrina and their father. "He likes to be called Android the Noid," she added, giving him a little hug.

Pulling out of his sister's embrace, Andrew said, "That was a long time ago, Katrina."

Mr. Gray chuckled. "Andrew is much more sophisticated now that he's nearly eleven. Where have you been anyway, Katrina? On the West Coast or something?"

Katrina laughed, but Leah detected a note of sadness in her laugh. "Yes, I guess I've probably missed a lot of changes at home, haven't I?"

"Not so many," her father said gently.

"Come on," Andrew urged. "Let's get going. I'm starved."

Katrina laughed again as she reached over to rumple her little brother's hair. "Some things never change, I guess."

"I'm hungry, too," Michael agreed. He had his arm around Annie's waist. Leah was trying not to be bothered by that fact, but it wasn't easy. She wanted to believe, now that they'd actually had a successful rehearsal, that Michael could have a crush on Annie and still dance well with her.

"We're going to stop on the way. I've made reservations at The Covered Bridge Inn. I thought Leah, in particular, would enjoy a New England dinner. Katrina tells me this is your first trip east, Leah," Mr. Gray said as he helped Kenny fit Leah's carryall into the back of the station wagon with the other luggage.

"Annie and Leah are from the same town in California, Daddy," Katrina said.

"Really? Then you girls must be old friends." Mr. Gray straightened up and looked from Leah to Annie and then back at Leah again.

Leah nodded. Honesty in a situation like this was pointless. "We used to go to the same ballet school. But then Annie left for New York when she was fourteen. We've only seen a little of each other since then—until now, that is."

"You went to New York alone when you were fourteen?" Mr. Gray asked as Katrina ducked into the backseat of the station wagon. Annie waited while Kenny slid in next to Katrina. Then she got in, too.

"I went with my mother. Then Mother went back to San Lorenzo after my sixteenth birthday." Annie chuckled. "I guess by then she was convinced I wasn't going to be devoured by big city wolves. Anyway, it's cheaper for me to share an apartment with three other girls than it was for my mother and me to live alone."

"Isn't that something? Sharing a one-bedroom apartment with three other girls!" Katrina exclaimed to Michael as he got in next to Annie. The backseat was full then. Leah had no choice but to sit up front between Katrina's father and brother.

"I've been looking forward to meeting you, Leah," Andrew said shyly as soon as the car was rolling down the street toward the road that would take them north to the valley where the Grays' farm was located.

"I've been looking forward to meeting you, too, Andrew. I think Katrina's very lucky to have a brother. I don't have a brother—or a sister, either," Leah told him, aware that a conversation about Annie's glamorous life in New York was going on behind her.

Andrew shook his head. At almost eleven he was nearly as tall as Leah herself. In fact, sitting down, she found herself eye to eye with him. He had the same soft brown eyes as his sister, and Leah could easily see that one day Andrew Gray was going to be a real heartbreaker.

"That must be kind of lonely," he said.

"Sometimes," Leah agreed. "But I have a dog named Pavlova and an orange cat named Misha, who keep me company. I also have a wonderful mother."

"But you don't live at home anymore, do you? You live with Katrina in San Francisco," Andrew pointed out.

"Yes, but my mother doesn't live as far away from San Francisco as you do. Sometimes I go home for the weekend, or she comes to San Francisco to visit me," Leah explained.

"Someday we're going to fly to San Francisco to visit Katrina," Andrew said proudly. "I guess we'll see you, too, while we're there, won't we?"

"I hope so," Leah said. She had an urge to give Andrew a hug, but somehow she didn't think ten-year-old boys were big on hugs. She was grateful to him for trying to talk with her. It made being ignored by the contingency in the backseat easier to bear.

"Well, here we are," Mr. Gray said, pulling the station wagon off the main road and parking in front of a charming old home.

"Remember the time we took that bicycle trip, Dad," Katrina said, leaning forward to hang over the front seat. "Didn't we stay here then?"

Mr. Gray nodded. "You've got a good memory, Kat. That was a long time ago."

"I remember this place, too," Andrew piped up.

Mr. Gray laughed. "Now that's truly amazing, Drew, because you were so little then that we left you with Grandma and Grandpa. Well, everybody out."

Leah was so enchanted by the cozy interior of the inn that for a moment she forgot she was the only girl there without a date. But she remembered as soon as Kenny and Michael held Katrina and Annie's chairs for them.

Leah must have looked bewildered because Andrew said, "Sit by me, Leah. Over here." Leah smiled and joined Andrew on the other side of the large round table from Katrina and Annie, who were sitting side by side.

Dinner was served family style, and since they'd been expected, their meal arrived shortly after they sat down.

"This is wonderful," Kenny said, enthusiastically spooning a mound of mashed-potato pie onto his plate.

"I thought you kids would enjoy a homey atmosphere," Mr. Gray said, offering Leah the platter of Yankee pot roast. "I'm only sorry Katrina's mother couldn't come with us. She had a meeting at Andrew's school that she felt she couldn't miss."

"I thought she didn't come because there wasn't going to be enough room in the car," Andrew protested.

"Andrew," Mr. Gray warned.

Andrew's pale face turned beet red as he realized what he'd said. But instead of looking at Annie, the true last-minute addition to this trip, Andrew focused his embarrassment on Leah. Leah felt her own cheeks grow hot as Mr. Gray passed her the basket of warm dinner rolls.

Of course Andrew would single Leah out from the others, she told herself, her eyes focused on her butter plate. Leah was the odd one out—the fifth wheel.

After dinner, as everyone was walking back to the car, Kenny winked at Leah. "You and Andrew make a handsome couple," he teased.

Leah forced herself to smile at Kenny's joke, even though she wasn't exactly in the mood to be teased. She decided it might be best all around if she tried to ignore Andrew as much as possible, beginning with the rest of the car trip.

But avoiding Andrew's attention proved easier than Leah had thought it would be. As soon as the old station wagon pulled out onto the main road again, Andrew fell asleep, with his head resting on Leah's shoulder.

Chapter 11

Wednesday morning Leah woke up stiff from her night on the narrow camp cot she'd agreed to sleep on while Katrina and Annie shared Katrina's double bed. All three girls had been in Katrina's room, but, isolated on the cot, Leah felt a universe away from them as they whispered and giggled together. She knew they were talking about Michael and Kenny, but she couldn't quite make out what they were saying. Trying had finally put her to sleep.

Leah sat up. Stretching her arms over her head, she yawned. Then, looking over at Katrina's bed, she was surprised to see that the other two girls were already up. The bed was even made. Leah was even more surprised when she went downstairs to find everyone, including the boys, dressed and eating breakfast already.

"Hurry up and get dressed, Leah," Andrew urged, waving a mug of hot chocolate at her. "We're all going to go swimming."

"Isn't it a little cold for swimming?" Leah asked, pulling the flannel robe she'd found in Katrina's closet more tightly around her.

"It'll warm up fast today. There isn't a cloud in the sky. Run along now," Mrs. Gray urged Leah with a wave of her spatula. "Your eggs will be ready in a couple of minutes."

Leah dressed quickly. She couldn't help feeling upset that it was Wednesday already. The auditions for the gala were the very next day. Leah wanted to suggest they skip the swim and get back to Greenfield early. That way they might even be able to work in another rehearsal.

"Here you go, Leah," Mrs. Gray said, handing Leah a plate of scrambled eggs and thick-sliced toast as soon as she stepped into the kitchen again.

"Thank you." Leah took the plate and sat down. Everyone else had apparently finished. The boys were nowhere in sight, and Annie and Katrina were at the kitchen counter making sandwiches.

The breakfast looked good, but Leah wasn't very hungry. Poking at the eggs, she said, "Don't you think we better head back to Greenfield now? The auditions are tomorrow, remember? If we get back early, we might be able to work in an extra rehearsal. Besides, Madame will be furious if we're late for that compulsory seminar this afternoon."

"We're going to go swimming at that pond I told you about, Leah," Katrina said. "It's a beautiful day, and it'll be a lot of fun."

"Anyway, we just got here," Annie pointed out.

"You'll be back in plenty of time," Mrs. Gray promised. "Katrina's father will see to that."

"Hi," Michael said cheerfully, coming back in the kitchen from outside.

"Where's Kenny?" Katrina asked.

"He's gone with Andrew to feed the chickens," Michael replied. "You have quite a farm here, Mrs. Gray."

The older woman smiled. "It's small, but Hal and I enjoy raising some of our own food."

"The picnic's ready!" Annie announced. She held up the picnic hamper she and Katrina had just filled for Michael to see.

Leah got up from the large table in the center of the Gray's kitchen and carried her plate to the sink. "I was just saying I thought we should go back early," Leah told Michael. "We've got that seminar later, and the auditions are tomorrow afternoon."

"We're going back after the picnic," Michael told her. Then he looked over at Katrina and Annie. "Right?" They nodded, and Leah sighed. She seemed to be outvoted again.

Just then Kenny and Andrew came running into the kitchen. They were both grinning. "I've decided that when I'm too old to dance anymore, I'm going to farm," Kenny announced.

Katrina's eyes widened. "You? I thought you were a city boy, Kenny."

"Your brother has converted me," Kenny told her.

"Aw, come on," Andrew protested, clearly pleased. "All we did was feed the chickens."

"Which were already fed once this morning," Mrs. Gray said, giving Andrew a knowing look.

"We just gave them a little more. Kenny wanted to, and he's a guest," Andrew pointed out.

"That's fine, Andrew," his mother assured him. "But don't you have some other real chores to do now?"

"But I'm going swimming," Andrew protested.

"Is that all right with you, Katrina?" Mrs. Gray asked, turning to her daughter. "Do you mind taking Andrew?"

Katrina smiled at her little brother. "Not at all. We'd like to have him along."

"Okay. I'm all set," Mr. Gray said, sticking his head in the kitchen window. "Put your suits on under your clothes—just in case it's not warm enough—and we'll go."

Minutes later, the Grays' old station wagon was stirring up a cloud of dust as they drove down the dirt road that joined their farm to the neighbors'. Then Mr. Gray stopped.

"This is as far as I can go with the car. But you know how to get to the clearing where the pond is from here, don't you, Kat?" Mr. Gray asked.

"I know," Andrew said proudly. "I can lead the way."

His father eyed him sternly. "Just remember what your mother and I told you last Wednesday, young man."

Andrew lowered his eyes. "I remember," he said solemnly.

As they piled out of the car, Leah realized that it was warming up fast. The bright sun made the woods smell fresh, and Leah began to look forward to swimming.

Katrina let Andrew lead the way. Michael carried the picnic hamper, and Kenny carried the blanket Mrs. Gray had insisted they take along to sit on. Leah brought up the rear.

It wasn't long before they reached a clearing. The pond reflected the clear blue sky above it and looked really inviting.

"Yahoo!" Kenny whooped, tossing the blanket aside and pulling off his shirt in one swift movement. "The last one in is a rotten egg!"

Then clothing started flying every which way.

Deciding to take her time about going in, Leah found a large rock to sit on while she took off her white sneakers.

She was about to take off her jeans when she realized someone was standing next to her. Startled, she straightened up.

"Hi," Andrew said shyly. "I thought maybe you were going to take a walk or something. I could come with you," he added hopefully, "you know, so you don't get lost."

"Actually I was just getting ready to go in," Leah told him. Then she smiled. "I bet you're a great swimmer."

Andrew shrugged. "Pretty good, I guess. But my dad won't let me come over here by myself."

"Aren't you going to swim, Leah?" Annie asked, joining them at the rock. Leah could hear Kenny, Michael, and Katrina splashing loudly in the water, but Annie wasn't undressed, either.

"Aren't you going swimming?" Leah countered. "Michael's already in the water," she added pointedly.

Annie rolled her eyes, apparently angered by Leah's statement. "I just thought if you weren't going to go in right away, I might sit here with you. Why are you so down on me anyway? I was actually glad to see you when I first got here, but now—"

"You've been going out of your way to make my life miserable, that's why," Leah interrupted. "You were friendly in the beginning, all right. But you've come between me and Katrina and made it awkward for Michael and me to dance well together. And now you're trying to act like there's something wrong with *me* for being upset about it." With that Leah picked up her bag and started walking back toward the Grays' house.

"Where are you going?" Annie demanded, hurrying after Leah.

"I'm going back. I shouldn't have come on this trip in the first place. I should have known it would be awful with you around," Leah said over her shoulder.

"Fine, go back to the farmhouse if you think it'll make you happy. Only this isn't the way we came," Annie informed Leah, still following her.

"Of course it is," Leah insisted, picking up her pace.

"No, it isn't."

Leah started running. "It is!" she shouted angrily over her shoulder.

"It is not!" Annie called out, running after her.

"Wait!" Andrew yelled. "Don't go that way!"

But Leah wasn't about to stop until Annie quit following her. She kept going, dodging branches and leaping over fallen trees. Then she stopped to catch her breath, and looked around her. The woods were thick, and the trail seemed to have ended. The road she was expecting to find was nowhere in sight.

"Well?" Annie demanded, coming up behind her. "If you're so smart, where are we now?"

Leah looked at Andrew, who was struggling to catch up with them. "This is the way back to your place, isn't it, Andrew?"

Andrew looked around uncertainly for a moment. Then he said, "I don't think this is a real trail." Then he looked up at the sky. A blanket of clouds had rolled in, hiding the sun. "If I could see the sun, I might be able to tell," he added.

"Of course this is a trail," Leah said. She looked back the way they'd come. Suddenly what she had thought was a trail didn't look like a trail anymore. She couldn't even tell for certain which direction she'd come from.

"I told you this wasn't the way." Annie sounded disgusted. "Now, let's go back before we all get lost. I won't even bother telling the others how stupid you've been, so you don't have to worry about looking bad again."

"Stupid!" Leah cried. "You're the one—" Then she stopped. Andrew was looking at her, wide-eyed. He seemed really frightened. "What's wrong?" Leah asked him gently.

Andrew looked down at his feet. "I don't want you guys to fight anymore."

"We're not fighting," Annie said. "Not really." She took several steps in Andrew's direction, then said, "Let's just turn around now and walk back the way we came. Come on. Follow me."

"Okay," Leah said, deciding to go along with Annie for Andrew's sake. But the threesome walked for a long time without getting back to the pond.

"Maybe if we yelled," Annie suggested. Then, without waiting for Leah's approval, she yelled, "Michael! Katrina!" But the woods only echoed Annie's cries.

"It's so cloudy." Andrew looked worried. "I think we're lost! My dad's going to be really mad at me."

Leah shivered as a chilly gust of wind rustled through the woods. It felt as if it might rain any moment. "Look, how lost can we be? I mean, this farm borders your farm, right, Andrew?"

Andrew nodded. "But only along one side.

There's a state forest on one side, too, and it goes on forever."

"But we'd come to a fence before that, wouldn't we?" Leah asked, trying not to panic.

"I don't know. We don't have fences all around our place. We don't need them. I mean, we don't have cows or anything like that to keep in." Andrew sank down to the ground.

"Oh, swell," Annie groaned, looking at her watch. "It's already noon. If we don't get out of here soon, we're going to miss that big seminar. Sandra Evans will have my hide if she finds out. The company paid for me to attend this festival, you know. So, for me it's like working."

"That's right," Leah retorted. "Rub in the fact that you're a professional dancer, while I'm still a student."

"When are you going to grow up, Leah? You're the lucky one. You've always been allowed to develop at your own pace, while I've been forced to move too fast. First it was my mother, and now it's the company."

"Please," Andrew wailed, wiping away a tear with the back of his hand. "There are wild animals in these woods. That's what my dad was warning me about when he dropped us off. I'm not allowed to go wandering around in here."

"Wild animals?" Leah and Annie said in unison. Then Leah added, "What kind of wild animals?"

"Squirrels and birds?" Annie asked hopefully.

Andrew nodded. "And bears."

"Bears!" Annie and Leah cried, exchanging a look of shock.

"Sure. There are lots of bears in the state forest. Sometimes they wander out onto someone's farm. That's why my dad doesn't let me go into the woods alone. Bears can get really mad if you get too close to one of their cubs, even if you don't mean to."

Just then Leah heard a rustle in the woods. "I heard something," she whispered.

"Maybe it's Michael," Annie suggested hopefully. "Michael?" Annie said tentatively as the noise came closer. "Is that you?"

"Aaahhhh!" All three of them screamed, diving into each other's arms as a doe followed by two spotted fawns leapt through the woods just a few yards in front of them.

"A deer!" Andrew said, smiling for the first time. "Three of them."

"They were beautiful." Annie sounded surprisingly reverent.

"And we're nuts," Leah told them both.

Then all three of them started laughing.

Chapter 12

Andrew sobered first. "There are still bears out here, you know. We were just lucky, that's all."

"And we're still lost," Annie pointed out, slumping slightly.

"True," Leah agreed. "But I think the best thing for us to do is stay put. If we keep wandering around, we might just get farther and farther away and more and more lost."

"You're right, Leah." Andrew nodded his head. "That's what my dad says, too."

Annie threw her hands up in the air. "Great. We're stuck here, waiting for bears who may or may not come." She looked down at her watch. "It's getting late. We're going to miss both the seminar and our rehearsal time if we don't get out of here soon."

"Well, there's nothing we can do about it now, is there?" Leah demanded. "We might as well make the most of it."

Annie sat down, her long legs out in front of her, and began doing warm-up stretches. "What do you suggest?" she asked as she took hold of the soles of her sneakers, bringing her chest to her knees.

"Well," Leah said thoughtfully, "we can tell stories."

Andrew nodded enthusiastically. "I love stories!"

"I don't know any stories," Annie complained.

"Of course you do, Annie. You know the stories of the ballets," Leah insisted.

"I know some of those stories," Andrew told them. "Katrina used to tell them to me when she still lived at home. But you two go first. I'm not sure if I remember them exactly right."

"I'll go first," Leah volunteered. "I'll tell the story of *Coppélia*. You'll like this story, Andrew. It has a strange old toymaker in it who makes life-like dolls."

"You mean like a mad scientist?" Andrew asked eagerly.

"Kind of like that," Leah agreed. Then she told the story of the girl with the enamel eyes, a doll so lifelike, she almost stole a real live boy away from a real live girl.

"I like that one," Andrew said as soon as Leah had finished. "I'm sure Katrina never told me that one before."

Annie shook her head. "Probably not. It's not exactly the best story."

"Tell a better one, why don't you?" Leah challenged.

"How about *Giselle*?" Annie asked "Do you know that story, Andrew?"

Andrew shook his head. "I don't think so. Tell it, Annie."

"It's too scary," Leah said with a shiver.

"Scary?" Andrew's eyes lit up.

Leah nodded. "It has ghosts in it."

"Ghosts don't frighten me anymore," Andrew declared bravely.

"I agree with Andrew. Bears are much more frightening than ghosts." Annie drew her legs up to her chest and began rocking back and forth.

Leah shrugged. "I'm outvoted, then. Go ahead, Annie."

"All right," Annie said, "I will." Then she proceeded to tell the story of Giselle, the beautiful young girl who kills herself when she discovers that the man she loves is really a prince, who can't marry her because she's only a peasant, and he has to marry a princess.

"That's not scary," Andrew complained when Annie paused for a moment in the story.

"Not yet, but that's only the first half," Annie told him. "The second half takes place in a spooky woods."

"Like these woods?" Andrew asked softly. His large brown eyes traveled nervously around the trees that towered above them.

Annie nodded. "*Just* like these woods, Andrew. Anyway, the prince comes to visit Giselle's grave in the woods. It's midnight, and the moon is full. He really did love Giselle, you see, and he misses her and her wonderful dancing terribly. Then, while he's there feeling sad, he sees something."

"A ghost?" Andrew asked, even more softly.

Annie nodded solemnly. "Yes," she said, "the ghost of the dead Giselle."

All at once there was a tremendous crash somewhere near them. Both Leah and Andrew screamed.

"There you are!" Michael cried, suddenly appearing through a tangle of underbrush. "Thank goodness you guys had the sense to stay in one place. Mr. Gray said if you kept walking, we might not be able to find you without more help. Did you know there are bears in these woods?"

"Oh, Michael," Annie said, throwing her arms around his neck. "I'm so glad to see you!"

"I'll say," Leah seconded.

Michael gave Annie a quick kiss. Then he pulled a whistle out of the pocket of his jeans and blew it.

"We'll wait here until the others find us," Michael told him. But they didn't have to wait longer than a minute or two before Kenny, Katrina, and Mr. Gray appeared.

"I hope this wasn't your doing, Andrew," Mr. Gray said, after giving his son a fierce hug.

"It was my fault, Mr. Gray," Leah said. "I was the one who thought I could walk back to your farm, without really knowing where I was going. Andrew was only trying to help me." Then Leah looked over at Annie, and it suddenly dawned on her that Annie had been trying to do the same thing. "And so was Annie," Leah added softly. Annie smiled at her.

"Well, no real harm's been done," Mr. Gray said. "Thank goodness for that."

"That's not exactly true, though," Michael said crossly. "Madame Preston is going to be furious with all of us for missing the seminar this afternoon, not to mention the last rehearsal we no longer have but all desperately need."

"We won't get back any earlier standing around complaining," Mr. Gray pointed out. "What's done is done."

"I don't care about Madame; I'm just glad everyone is all right," Katrina insisted, giving Andrew,

Leah, and Annie each a hug as they started back through the woods. "Anyway, I'm sure Madame Preston will understand."

But Leah wasn't sure. Madame had said when they had asked permission to go to Katrina's back in San Francisco that it was all right under one condition. They absolutely had to be back for the seminar. And when Madame said *absolutely*, she meant it!

When the old station wagon finally started up the main street of Greenfield, Mr. Gray cleared his throat, breaking the spell of silence that the car had been under for the entire trip back. "I hope everyone has learned a lesson," he said sternly, "especially Leah and Annie. Unfamiliar woods can be dangerous. You girls were wrong to expect a ten-year-old boy to be your guide.

"I think they realize that now, Dad," Katrina assured her father.

"I hope so," Mr. Gray said as he turned into the Greenfield College parking lot.

"Oh, oh," Michael groaned. "There's Madame Preston!"

"It looks like she's waiting for someone," Kenny said. "And she doesn't look very happy."

"Bryce Coleman and Sandra Evans are with her, too," Annie pointed out, sounding alarmed. "They're both from my company."

"I had my wife call to let everyone know where you were," Mr. Gray told them. "I'm sure they're waiting for you."

Andrew snickered. "And I thought *I* was in trouble."

"Now, Andrew," Mr. Gray cautioned, stopping the car.

"What's the meaning of this?" Madame demanded in her sternest voice as soon as everyone was out of the car. "Do you realize you've missed the mandatory seminar?"

Everyone, including Leah, nodded.

"Well, I'm going to leave you kids," Mr. Gray said, ushering a wide-eyed Andrew back into the station wagon. "Has everyone got everything?"

There was more nodding and a chorus of soft thank-yous; then Mr. Gray and Andrew left.

"The seminar you've missed was not optional," Madame said. "I reminded you of that when I gave you permission to go to Katrina's in the first place. You haven't kept your word to me, and I'm very disappointed in all of you."

Leah and the others apologized. But as soon as Leah had said she was sorry, she realized that a mere apology wasn't going to be enough for Madame Preston.

"I'm afraid I'm going to have to take disciplinary action. I don't know what Mr. Coleman and Ms. Evans intend to do with Annie, but I've decided that you four must lose the privilege of auditioning for the special festival performance."

"But that's not fair!" Leah cried before she could stop herself.

"I realize this punishment may seem harsh," Madame said firmly, "but you need to learn the importance of discipline. If you hope to be part of a professional dance company one day, many people, including your fellow dancers, the audience, and the patrons will be relying on you to meet your commitments."

"I mean, it was my fault that we got back late," Leah said as soon as it was clear that Madame had finished speaking her mind. "*I'm* the one who got lost in the woods. Kenny, Michael, and Katrina had no choice but to stay until we were found."

"Is this true?" Madame asked.

"Yes," Leah answered quickly

"All right. Only Leah will sit out the auditions, then," Madame said.

"Being late tonight was as much my fault as Leah's. I followed her into the woods. If Leah's going to be punished, I ought to be, too." Leah stared at Annie, unable to believe that the Annie she thought she knew was capable of so noble a gesture.

"But Annie!" Michael cried. "What about our pas de deux?"

"It was my fault that Annie got lost," Leah admitted before Annie could say anything else. "*I* was the one who wandered away from where we were supposed to be. Annie only followed me to keep me from getting lost. Unfortunately she got lost, too."

Sandra Evans, who had been silent up until now, took a step forward. "I am as interested in fairness as anyone else here," she began. "And I'm upset with Annie's disregard for the required seminar. But the company has paid for Annie to come here to dance. While giving up the audition may be right for Leah, Annie, as a professional, will have to be disciplined in a different way. I'm afraid, Annie, that for your part in this unfortunate escapade, you will be fined a hundred dollars."

Annie let out a little gasp, but she didn't protest.

"Now, if you hurry," Bryce said, "you may be

able to find an open practice room where you can rehearse. Auditions, if you haven't forgotten, are tomorrow."

"Leah, wait!" Annie called as soon as Madame and the others began to walk away in their separate directions.

"I'll see you back in our room, Leah," Katrina said. Then she hurried away, leaving Annie and Leah alone.

"You took the blame," Annie said simply.

Leah nodded. "So did you. You didn't have to do that, you know. A hundred dollars is a lot of money."

Annie shrugged. "I'm not happy about that, but I do feel good about speaking up. Besides, I was as much to blame as you. If I hadn't goaded you on the way, you wouldn't have felt compelled to run off and escape from me."

"But I thought you followed me to help me. Didn't you?" Leah asked.

Annie shrugged again. "Maybe. I'm not really sure what was on my mind. Anyway, you've been right about a lot of things, Leah. When we were younger, you always had the things I never did, like a mother who really loved you for who you were instead of who she wanted you to be. You also had friends, good friends. I think I would have traded being Clara in *The Nutcracker* for your mother or a friend like Chrissy Morely."

"But wasn't Elinore Kingston your friend?" Leah asked. "I always thought you two were really close."

Annie shook her head. "No, not really. We were for a while, I suppose, but my mother quickly put an end to that. You see, Elinore started dancing too well. And yet, my mother never let me have girls who weren't dancers for friends, either. You still write to Chrissy, don't you?" Annie asked wistfully. "You told me that first morning you do."

Leah nodded. "I've gotten two letters since we've been here."

"And Katrina's your friend, too. So are Michael and Kenny. You probably have friends all over the place. Anyway, seeing you again brought back all those feelings, especially when you saw me that first night but pretended you hadn't. I felt I had to prove that I was just as nice—maybe even nicer than you."

Annie's words made Leah feel even worse than she had. "You're right, Annie. I did see you, but I didn't follow you," she admitted. "I'm really sorry I didn't at least give you a chance to show me that you'd changed."

"And I'm sorry I was so quick to take offense, so eager to get even with you for that slight."

"You mean you were trying to steal Katrina and Michael's friendships away from me?" Leah asked.

"At first," Annie confessed. "But then something really did happen, something I never planned. I really like Katrina, and I think I'm really in love with Michael. You believe me, don't you, Leah?"

Leah nodded. "I didn't, but I do now."

"I've never danced with anyone the way I dance with Michael. We're really in tune with each other." Annie's eyes took on a dreamy, faraway look. "If it isn't love, it's the closest I've ever come to it."

"I've always been jealous of you," Leah explained. "When we were younger, it seemed like every time I figured out what the next thing to go after was, you were already there, walking away with the honors. I guess I feel like I've spent a lot of my life eating your dust. I never thought until now that you might want anything *I* had."

"Do you think we can ever be friends?" Annie asked. Her eyes searched Leah's face hopefully.

"I don't really know," Leah admitted honestly. "We can certainly stop being enemies, though."

"Do you think you can wish me luck at the audition tomorrow?" Annie looked eagerly at Leah. "It means a lot to me, Leah, and I know it would mean a lot to Michael, too."

Leah couldn't help thinking that her punishment for their escapade in the woods was much worse than Annie's. She'd gladly pay a hundred dollars for the privilege of auditioning for the gala. But Leah also knew that as far as Madame was concerned, the matter was closed. That wasn't Annie's fault. Annie could just as easily have kept quiet once Leah had offered to shoulder all the blame, but she hadn't. And Annie had been punished for it. Leah didn't need to punish her more.

"Good luck," Leah said. And she really meant it, too.

Chapter 13

Leah was already sitting down on
the lawn that rimmed the Greenfield Performing
Arts Center, even though the special Sunday performance wouldn't begin for another half hour.
Only general admission tickets had been left by
the time Leah knew she wouldn't be dancing herself, and she'd come early to be sure to get a
good view of the stage.

Even though she had been banned from partici-
pating in the auditions, she'd gone to watch them.
She wasn't at all surprised when both Kenny and
Katrina and Michael and Annie had won a place on
the program. If the performance today was even half
as good as the auditions had been, Leah knew the
gala was going to be a huge success.

Leah was scanning the crowd when she spotted Alexandra Sorokin, her Russian friend who
had dropped out of SFBA earlier in the year. She'd
actually been looking for Alex since Friday, when
a sweatshirt with a funky picture of the Statue of
Liberty had arrived, along with the cryptic mes-
sage, "See you soon. Love, Alex." Besides, Kay
had mentioned that Alex might be coming to
Greenfield, since she was in New York with her
parents for the summer. Leah gave up her spot

on the lawn and hurried after the raven-haired girl.

"Alex!" Leah cried. "Alex, wait!"

Alex was dressed in a white cotton eyelet dress, her sleek black hair cascading down her back luxuriously. As usual, she looked beautiful.

"Leah, what are you doing here? Should you not be backstage now?" Alex exclaimed, her dark eyes clouding with concern even as she rushed to the blond girl's side. "I did not expect to see you until after the performance."

As soon as Alex was close enough, Leah threw her arms around her and gave her an enormous hug. "I'm so glad you're here, Alex! I danced in the corps last night, but I'm not dancing today," she confessed softly. Then she brightened. "But Katrina, Kenny, and Michael are."

"How is it that they are and you are not?" Alex asked. "You have not hurt yourself again, have you?" She glanced down at Leah's leg.

Leah shook her head. "No. It's a long story, though, and kind of awkward. I'll tell you later," she promised. "That is, if you're interested."

"You are my friend," Alex declared. "Naturally I am interested. But I will wait to hear your story."

"Thanks. Are your parents with you?" She had met Alex's parents, famous international ballet stars, a couple of times before and had always enjoyed them.

Alex shook her head. "My parents wanted to come but had much work keeping them back in New York. They found a ride for me instead with an old family friend." Alex smiled. "Maybe you have heard of this man, Leah. He used to be a danseur but is now fund-raiser for many small companies in both the United States and England. Nicholas Weatherby is his name."

"You're kidding!" Leah shrieked, her hands flying to her mouth. "That's wonderful!"

"It is? You know this man?" Alex's almost-black, almond-shaped eyes registered surprise. "I must confess I had not heard of him until my parents arranged for me to come up here with him. He is English. That is where my parents met him, in England."

"He danced with Svetlana Lobinskya. She's really English, you know, despite her Russian name," Leah explained. "In fact, it was Nicholas Weatherby who helped her decide to change her name from Mabel Terwilliger."

Alex chuckled. "I think maybe I know why she changed a name like that to a proud Russian name like Svetlana."

"Miss Lobinskya said something else. She told us she fell in love with almost all of her partners, but her *first* love was the best ... even though she didn't realize it until later. I think that Nicholas Weatherby was that first love! Maybe they'll even rediscover each other here today. Wouldn't that be romantic?"

Alex shook her head. "You never change, Leah. You think too much of romance. This gets you into trouble, I think."

"You might be right," Leah agreed. Then she added, "The orchestra is tuning up now. I think we better find a place to sit. Madame Preston warned me that there's no limit on the number of general admission tickets sold."

"Do not worry. My parents bought three reserved seats as soon as this performance was announced, hoping the three of us would be able to come together. You must sit with Mr. Weatherby and me, Leah," Alex insisted.

"Look, Alex!" Leah cried, forgetting her manners as she pointed in front of them. "There's Miss Lobinskya. Is that man talking to her Mr. Weatherby?"

Alex laughed as she pulled Leah's finger down. "Do not point, Leah. It is rude! But you are right. That is Mr. Weatherby."

Leah sighed contentedly. "They've found each other, then."

Alex nodded. "Yes, they do seem happy."

"Maybe I shouldn't sit with you after all," Leah said, holding back for a moment. "Maybe if I don't go down there with you, they'll sit together."

But Alex refused to let Leah go back to the lawn. "I am sure Miss Lobinskya has her own seat, probably the best seat of all. She can see Mr. Weatherby after the performance. We are not going back to New York until tonight, after the big party."

By the time the girls reached their seats, Miss Lobinskya had left and Mr. Weatherby was sitting down. Alex introduced them, but Leah wasn't able to say much of anything to the distinguished-looking older man before the curtain opened on the first dance, the same pas de trois from _Swan Lake_ that Leah had danced with Pam and Kenny in a student production earlier that year. As Leah watched, she could easily imagine herself up on the stage dancing every little echappé, entrechat, and jump on pointe.

The pas de trois was followed by a solo, the wonderful Bluebird variation from _The Sleeping_

Beauty. Once again Leah, having performed this variation herself at one time, performed in her mind each of the cabrioles, front and back, and the numerous entrechats right along with the girl on stage.

Later, as Kenny and Katrina danced Siegfried and Odette's moving pas de deux from the second act of *Swan Lake,* Alex leaned toward Leah and said, "Is that really Kenny Rotolo?"

Leah nodded. Then she watched as Katrina turned slowly on pointe with Kenny's support. Katrina looked every bit the enchanted swan, while Kenny looked earthly and strong.

Hearing Alex click her tongue softly, Leah turned her eyes from the stage and focused questioningly on her friend. "More romance?" Alex whispered in a teasing voice. Leah decided it would be better if she let Katrina tell Alex how she felt about Kenny. In fact, Leah told herself as she joined in the thunderous applause that greeted the conclusion of Kenny and Katrina's dance, she wasn't going to say another word to Alex about anyone's romance if she could help it.

During the brief intermission that followed, Mr. Weatherby excused himself. Once they were alone, Leah told Alex about the fiasco at the Grays' farm that had ended in her losing the privilege to audition for the performance.

Alex shook her head. "Once again your own imagination has proved to be your worst enemy, Leah."

Leah nodded. "I know I shouldn't have let Annie bother me the way I did. But she did confess, after we got back, that she really had gone out of her way to make things hard for me. I was right all along. She was as jealous of *me* as I've always been of *her*."

"Very childish of both of you," Alex said matter-of-factly. "But now I think you realize you are no longer children. You must put aside petty jealousies, no? Remember what I told you, Leah. The world of ballet is very small, perhaps too small. You and Annie must learn to share that small world, or you both will suffer for it. You will say good-bye to Annie at the end of Summer Dance, but it will not be good-bye forever."

"You're right, Alex, and I see that now. Anyway, wait until you see Michael dance with Annie. You won't believe it. Annie taught him the second-act pas de deux from *Giselle* in just a few days."

Alex's pencil-thin eyebrows shot up. "This Annie is dancing with Michael Litvak, your partner?"

Leah felt her cheeks grow warm. She didn't want to be jealous of Annie anymore, but she was anyway. Not quite as jealous as she'd once been, of course, but still jealous. Leah knew that Michael had never really been hers to begin with, but in her heart it still felt as if Annie had somehow stolen him away from her. Michael had grown to be a wonderful partner over the past year.

"Well, yes," Leah finally answered. She didn't want to say that Annie and Michael had fallen in love, not after the teasing she'd been getting about her preoccupation with love.

With a wry smile playing at her full lips, Alex said, "Go ahead, Leah. I know you die to tell me something."

"That's *dying* to tell you," Leah corrected Alex, laughing in spite of herself, "and I guess you're right. Annie and Michael are in love."

Alex shook her head sadly. "Poor Leah! No wonder you have a hard time here. Everyone at Summer Dance is in love but you!"

Before Leah could agree, Mr. Weatherby rejoined them, and the orchestra began tuning up, signaling the end of the intermission.

Michael and Annie's pas de deux was the last dance of the program, the place of honor. And their dance, full of sustained lifts and many beautiful développés, was incredibly moving.

"Leah," Alex said as both girls applauded Michael and Annie's performance, "you are crying!"

"Wasn't it wonderful, Alex?" Leah said, smiling, though her tears continued falling.

Alex returned Leah's smile. "Yes. Michael is much improved, I think, and your friend has a certain quality about her. It is a quality of tragedy, maybe, as if she understands what it is to suffer a great loss."

"Come on, girls," Mr. Weatherby said, leaning toward them. "I promised Mabel we'd give her a lift."

Leah laughed. "You mean Miss Lobinskya, don't you?"

Mr. Weatherby smiled fondly. "To you and the rest of the world she's Miss Lobinskya. But to me she'll always be little Mabel Terwilliger. We go way back, you know."

Leah looked at Alex and winked as she said, "Yes, we know."

In all too short a time they had arrived at the Ado estate where Miss Lobinskya lived and where the closing ceremony and farewell party were to take place. Mr. Weatherby dropped the girls at the splendid Ado garden; then he and Miss Lobinskya continued on up the dirt road to her cottage, promising before they pulled away that they'd see the girls again shortly.

"I suppose you will now tell me that Miss Lobinskya and Mr. Weatherby are in love," Alex teased as the girls strolled along the main path of the garden.

"I honestly don't know," Leah confessed. "The backseat of Mr. Weatherby's car was too far from the front seat, and you kept asking me questions on top of that."

Alex raised her perfectly tweezed eyebrows. "Leah Stephenson!" she cried. "Were you trying to eavesdrop?"

"Oh, look!" Leah commanded, hoping to change the subject. "There's the Greenfield College van. Let's go see if Katrina is here."

With a shrug Alex followed Leah back toward the parking lot. As soon as the van doors opened, Katrina jumped out.

"Alexandra! So you did come!" she cried, giving her a big hug.

"You knew I was coming?" Alex asked. She looked over at Leah, and Leah nodded.

"Kay mentioned that you were thinking about coming in her letters to both of us," Leah confessed. "She also asked us not to tell you that she told us."

Katrina's hand flew to her mouth. "Oops!"

"It is not your fault, Katrina, it is mine. I should have known better than to ask Kay Larkin to keep a secret," Alex assured Katrina. All three girls shared a good laugh. As they all knew, Kay was an incurable gossip. "And anyway," Alex added, "I did send Leah a clue. Did you like the sweatshirt?"

"I loved it!" Leah told her. "Thanks."

"Hey, look who's here," Kenny said. He gave Alex a quick kiss on the cheek. "Did you see the show, Alex?"

"I did," Alex replied. "You two dance well together."

Kenny slipped his arm around Katrina. "Thanks," he said. "It feels right."

Katrina blushed slightly as she tipped her head to the side and gave Kenny a warm smile. "I still can't believe we got to perform today. It's like a dream come true, especially since my family was able to see us." Then she quickly looked over at Leah. "Oh, Leah, I'm so sorry," she said hastily.

Leah forced herself to smile. "That's okay. I'm used to the idea by now. Anyway, I got to sit with Alex and—you aren't going to believe this, Katrina—Mr. Weatherby!"

"Nicholas Weatherby is here!" Katrina exclaimed.

Leah nodded. "He's up at Miss Lobinskya's cottage with her right now."

"Maybe he's proposing to her," Katrina suggested hopefully.

"You are both too much," Alex proclaimed with a shake of her head.

Katrina giggled. "But you don't know the whole story."

"You are wrong, Katrina. Leah has told me *everything*," Alex assured her.

"Everything?" Katrina asked, looking from Alex to Leah.

"Not everything," Leah insisted. "But where are

Annie and Michael? Weren't they in the van with you?" Leah looked past Kenny at the van.

"They were about to get in the van with the rest of us when Madame Preston and Bryce Coleman stopped them. The four of them were still standing in the parking lot talking when the van pulled away," Kenny informed them.

"Bryce Coleman is with the New York City Ballet, no?" Alex asked.

"That's right, Alex," Leah told her. "He's been teaching here for the past two weeks."

"Let's find the food," Katrina said. "I'm starving."

"Good idea," Kenny agreed.

"You two go ahead," Leah told them. "Alex and I will meet you in a few minutes."

After Kenny and Katrina walked away, Alex turned to face Leah. "I am hungry myself. Why are we waiting here?"

"There's something I haven't told you yet, Alex. Annie has been talking about arranging an audition for Michael with the New York City Ballet. She's even been suggesting that this performance might be an audition."

"Really?" Alex sounded impressed. Then she frowned. "Is something wrong? Why are you looking worried, Leah?"

"I'm worried about Michael. I'm afraid Annie's got him all excited about nothing."

"Look!" Alex cried. "There is Madame Preston, getting out of a car."

Leah followed Alex's gaze and saw that Michael and Annie were getting out of the same white limousine that Madame Preston had been riding in. Then Bryce Coleman and Sandra Evans got out as well.

"Now I think we will know," Alex said. "Come, Leah. I must say hello to Madame Preston before she goes away."

Reluctantly Leah followed Alex over to the gathering.

"Alexandra!" Madame said cheerfully, taking the Russian girl's hands in her own. "How wonderful to see you, my dear. Let me introduce you to Bryce Coleman and Sandra Evans from City Ballet. This is Alexandra Sorokin, the daughter of Olga and Dmitri Sorokin."

"Alexandra," Bryce said, taking her hand and giving it a kiss. "I'm charmed. I have always enjoyed watching your parents dance."

Alex looked pleased. "Thank you," she said graciously.

"Ms. Sorokin," Ms. Evans said, nodding her head at Alex. "I've heard some interesting things about your own dancing."

Leah didn't have long to wonder if Alex would say she'd given up ballet when she left SFBA earlier that year. She knew that Alex was still taking class every morning, even though she was a student at Berkeley now. But Alex didn't say anything about quitting. Instead, she merely said, "Thank you, Ms. Evans. I have also heard your name mentioned frequently, always with much respect."

"I'm not sure you know Annie MacPhearson, Alex," Madame said, drawing Annie into the circle. "But of course you know Michael Litvak."

As Leah watched Annie and Michael greet Alex, she knew that whatever had been discussed on their ride to Ado had pleased them both. Leah could barely wait until the introductions were over to find out what that was.

"Well?" Leah finally demanded as soon as there was a pause in the conversation.

Surprisingly, it was Madame Preston who spoke up. "Michael has been offered a contract with the New York City Ballet. He is going to apprentice with the company."

"Michael is moving to New York!" Annie squealed delightedly. "Isn't that wonderful, Leah?"

Leah was speechless. Remembering Madame's reaction to the movie offer she'd received the year before, Leah was shocked that Madame was so approving of this sudden, quite major move on Michael's part. Madame must have thought Michael was ready. Leah didn't want to feel jealous of that, but it was hard not to. Now not only was Michael getting a break, he was going to be able to continue dancing with Annie, which was undeniably a break for Annie as well. Leah couldn't help wondering if she'd ever catch up to her childhood rival. She knew that it shouldn't matter to her, but it did.

"Yes, it's wonderful," Leah finally agreed, forcing herself to smile first at Michael, then at Annie. After all, she was really happy for them both. "Congratulations, Michael. And congratulations to you, too, Annie."

"Thank you, Leah. Hey, I'm starved!" Michael declared, patting his well-muscled stomach tenderly. "All this excitement, you know."

Madame chuckled. "Boys! They are always hungry, aren't they?"

"Lead the way, Michael," Bryce commanded. "I

think I saw tables of food by the fountain on the other side of the garden."

As the group headed toward the buffet tables, Alex and Leah hung back with Madame Preston.

"Have you seen Svetlana, Leah?" Madame Preston asked.

"She's with Mr. Weatherby," Leah said.

Madame's usually stern face suddenly glowed with warmth. "Nick Weatherby is *here*?"

"He drove me up," Alex explained. "He is a friend of my parents."

Still smiling, Madame shook her head. "Ah, what a lovely end to Summer Dance! Don't you girls agree?"

Alex said, "It is a happy ending, I think."

Madame nodded. Then she seemed to notice that Leah wasn't sharing her enthusiasm for the way things seemed to have worked out.

"Don't worry, Leah," Madame said gently. "Even though you didn't dance today, you've been noticed. You'll get your chance one day, my dear."

Madame's words made Leah feel better than she had in a long time. She was about to thank her for her encouragement when she saw a familiar station wagon pull into the Ado parking lot.

"Leah!" Andrew Gray cried, leaping from the car as soon as it had stopped.

"Who is that little boy?" Alex asked, as the three of them watched Andrew race toward them.

"*My* summer romance, I'm afraid!" Leah promptly replied.

Then Leah and Alex both burst out laughing.

GLOSSARY

Adagio Slow tempo dance steps; essential to sustaining controlled body line. When dancing with a partner, the term refers to support of ballerina.

Allegro Quick, lively dance step.

Arabesque Dancer stands on one leg and extends the other leg straight back while holding the arms in graceful positions.

Arabesque penchée The dancer's whole body leans forward over the supporting leg. (Also referred to as penché.)

Assemblé A jump in which the two feet are brought together in the air before the dancer lands on the ground in fifth position.

Attitude turns The *attitude* is a classical position in which the working or raised leg is bent at the knee and extended to the back, as if wrapped around the dancer. An *attitude turn* is a turn performed in this position.

Ballon Illusion of suspending in air.

Barre The wooden bar along the wall of every ballet studio. Work at the barre makes up the first part of practice.

Battement Throwing the leg as high as possible into the air to the front, the side, and the back. Several variations.

Battement en cloche Swinging the leg as high as possible to the back and to the front to loosen the hip joint.

Batterie A series of movements in which the feet are beaten together.

Grande batterie Refers to steps with high elevation.

Petite batterie Steps with small elevation.

Bourrée Small, quick steps usually done on toes. Many variations.

Brisé A jump off one foot in which the legs are beaten together in the air.

Cabriole A step in which the dancer extends one leg to the front, back or side, and, springing upwards, brings the second leg up to the first before landing.

Centre work The main part of practice; performing steps on the floor after barre work.

Chaîné A series of short, usually fast turns on pointe by which a dancer moves across the stage.

Corps de ballet   Any and all members of the ballet who are not soloists.

Dégagé   Extension with toe pointed in preparation for a ballet step.

Demi-pointe   Half pointe.

Developpé   The slow raising and unfolding of one leg until it is high in the air (usually done in pas de deux, or with support of barre or partner).

Divertissement   A series of entertaining and/or technically brilliant dances performed within a ballet. For example, as in the Marzipan dance of *The Nutcracker* or in the Bluebird Variation in the last act of *The Sleeping Beauty*.

Echappé   A movement in which the dancer springs up from fifth position onto pointe in second position. Also a jump.

Enchaînement   A sequence of two or more steps.

Entrechat   A spring into the air from the fifth position in which the extended legs (with feet well pointed) criss-cross at the lower calf.

Fouetté   A step in which the dancer is on one leg and uses the other leg in a sort of whipping movement to help the body turn.

Frappé (or *battement frappé*)   A barre exercise in which the dancer extends the foot of the working leg to the front, side and back, striking the ball of the foot on the ground. Dancer then stretches the toe until it is slightly off the ground and returns the foot *sur le cou-de-pieds* (on the ankle) against the ankle of the supporting leg.

Glissade   A gliding step across the floor.

Jêté   A jump from one foot onto the other in which working leg appears to be thrown in the air.

Jêté en tournant   A jêté performed while turning.

Mazurka   A Polish national dance.

Pas de deux   Dance for 2 dancers. ("Pas de trois" means dance for 3 dancers, and so on.)

Pas de chat   Meaning "step of the cat." A light, springing movement. The dancer jumps and draws one foot up to the knee of the opposite leg, then draws up the other leg, one after the other, traveling diagonally across the stage.

Penché   Referring to an arabesque penchée.

Piqué   Direct step onto pointe without bending the knee of the working leg.

Plié   With feet and legs turned out, a movement by which the dancer bends both knees outward over her toes, leaving her heels on the ground.

Demi plié   Bending the knees as far as possible leaving the heels on the floor.

Grand plié Bending knees all the way down letting the heels come off the floor (except in second position).

Pointe work Exercises performed in pointe (toe) shoes.

Port de bras Position of the dancer's arms.

Posé Stepping onto pointe with a straight leg.

Positions There are five basic positions of the feet and arms that all ballet dancers must learn.

Relevé Raising of the body on full or half pointe.

Rétiré Drawing the toe of one foot to the opposite knee.

Rond de jambe a terre An exercise performed at the barre to loosen the hip joint: performed first outward (*en dehors*) and then inward (*en dedans*). The working leg is extended first to the front with the foot fully pointed and then swept around to the side and back and through first position to the front again. The movement is then reversed, starting from the fourth position back and sweeping around to the side and front. (The foot traces the shape of the letter "D" on the floor.)

Sissonné With a slight plié, dancer springs into the air from the fifth position, and lands on one foot with a demi plié with the other leg extended to the back, front, or side. The foot of the extended leg is then closed to the supporting foot.

Tendu Stretching or holding a certain position or movement.

Tour en l'air A spectacular jump in which the dancer leaps directly upwards and turns one, two or three times before landing.

Turn à la seconde Turn with the working leg raised off the floor in second position.

ABOUT THE AUTHOR

ELIZABETH BERNARD has had a lifelong passion for dance. Her interest and background in ballet is wide and various and has led to many friendships and acquaintances in the ballet and dance world. Through these connections she has had the opportunity to witness firsthand a behind-the-scenes world of dance seldom seen by non-dancers. She is familiar with the stuff of ballet life: the artistry, the dedication, the fierce competition, the heartaches, the pains, and the disappointments. She is the author of over two dozen books for young adults, including titles in the bestselling COUPLES series, published by Scholastic, and the SISTERS series, published by Fawcett.